'You're Pregnant With My Child. I Think That Means There's Something Going On Between Us.'

Hank cupped Susan's face between his two big hands. 'I've tried to deny the attraction. But trying to ignore it isn't going to make it go away.'

'Please.' Tears gathered in her eyes. 'Please don't do this.'

He kissed her forehead. 'Do you think I want to feel this way?' He kissed one of her cheeks and then the other. She trembled from head to toe. 'Do you think it's easy for me to admit that I want my best friend's widow?'

Susan opened her mouth to speak, but all that came out was a choked gasp.

'You want me, too, don't you, honey?' He urged her face upward until she met his gaze. 'You're as hungry for me as I am for you.'

Dear Reader,

Welcome to Desire™. As usual, we have six books sure to take your mind off those pesky April showers!

Wheeler Rush is our MAN OF THE MONTH, sweeping Audrey Finnegan off her feet in *That Boss of Mine*. She's temping at his office, but wants to stay *permanently* in Wheeler's arms!

Beverly Barton returns with the second instalment of 3 BABIES FOR 3 BROTHERS—a pregnant beauty, a rugged lawman: a recipe for success! And those McCLOUD BRIDES are back! In fact, *That McCloud Woman*, Alayna, has Jack Cordell practically down on one knee and *begging* her to marry him!

In *Single Female (Reluctantly) Seeks…* JeanAnn Turner finds love nearer to home than she imagined. And finally, in *The Billionaire's Secret Baby* and *The Cowboy and the Virgin* we meet two couples who find their attraction to each other too hot to handle…

Enjoy!

The Editors

His Woman, His Child

BEVERLY BARTON

SILHOUETTE

DESIRE

*Silhouette, Silhouette Desire and Colophon
are registered trademarks of Harlequin Books S.A.,
used under licence.*

*First published in Great Britain 2000
Silhouette Books, Eton House, 18-24 Paradise Road,
Richmond, Surrey TW9 1SR*

© Beverly Beaver 1999

ISBN 0 373 76209 7

22-0004

*Printed and bound in Spain
by Litografia Rosés S.A., Barcelona*

BEVERLY BARTON

has been in love with romance since her grandfather gave her an illustrated book of *Beauty and the Beast*. An avid reader since childhood, she began writing at the age of nine and wrote short stories, poetry, plays and novels throughout school and college. After marriage to her own 'hero' and the births of her daughter and son, she chose to be a full-time homemaker, a.k.a. wife, mother, friend and volunteer.

Beverly considers writing romance books a real labour of love. Her stories come straight from the heart, and she hopes that all the strong and varied emotions she invests in her books will be felt by everyone who reads them.

In loving memory of Christine Byrd Hardin,
who had a passion for books.
And to precious little Hannah Christine Files,
named in honour of her great-grandmother.

One

I'm pregnant.

Hank could hear Susan's voice inside his head, telling him the one thing he hadn't wanted to hear. He'd been so sure the first try hadn't been successful, that fate wouldn't be so cruel.

When he'd arrived at the funeral home last night and gone straight to her—his best friend's widow—she had taken his hand and squeezed it firmly.

"Thank you for coming, Hank," she had said, her voice quivering. "Lowell loved you like a brother."

Pain had sliced through him as if he'd been stabbed with a dull blade. But he hadn't flinched. Holding Susan's hand securely in his, he'd wished he could think of something—anything—to say that would lessen her sorrow. But there were no words to soothe the agony of a woman who had just lost her husband.

"Lowell was the finest man I've ever known," he had told her. "I'd have done anything for him."

"Yes, I know."

Their gazes locked and held, the unspoken message a secret each held within their hearts. They had both loved Lowell. They had both wanted to give him the one thing he'd longed for and couldn't have.

With her hand still in his, Susan had led Hank aside, leaned close and whispered in his ear, "I'm pregnant. We just found out two days ago. Lowell tried several times to call you."

Hank had felt his muscles freeze, his heartbeat accelerate. His mind had screamed, *No. A thousand times no. Not now.* Not when Lowell wouldn't be around to take care of Susan and the child.

"I was away on an assignment," he'd told her.

Before he could comment further on her announcement, Crooked Oak's mayor had grasped his shoulder. "Damn shame about Lowell. A finer man never lived. We're all going to miss him."

Now, as he stood with Lowell's family and friends at the grave site, the October wind whipped through the nearby trees, flapping the partially bare branches and loosening the dying foliage. The colorful autumn leaves flew across the cemetery like birds in flight. Thunder boomed in the distance. A fine mist of rain moistened the canopy under which those close to the deceased had congregated to say their final farewells.

Numbness had encased Hank ever since his brother Caleb had phoned to tell him that Lowell Redman had been murdered—killed in the line of duty as sheriff of Marshall County. Although he hadn't lived in Crooked Oak since he'd graduated from high school, Hank had remained best friends with Lowell. He'd even been best man at Lowell's wedding to Susan two years ago.

Susan. Sweet, quiet, gentle Susan. He'd thought she and Lowell a perfect match. Both good people.

She had asked him to sit with her today, but he had declined, using the excuse that the other ladies attending should be the ones seated. He stood across from her, on the opposite side of Lowell's casket. She sat stiffly, her face pale, her hands clutched tightly in her lap. Dear God, the pain she must be suffering!

Every instinct within him wanted to reach out to her, to pull her into his arms and hold her. Comfort her. Assure her that she wasn't alone. To promise that he would take care of her.

But how would she react if he touched her? More importantly, how would he react? Knowing she was pregnant brought all his primeval, protective instincts to the surface.

He'd known Susan Williams Redman all her life. She'd been one of his sister Tallie's best friends. But back then he'd never thought of her as anything but a quiet, shy, plain little girl who used to stare at him with big blue eyes. Then he'd seen her at Tallie's wedding several years ago and realized that the plain little girl had grown into a lovely young woman. If she hadn't been dating Lowell at the time, he would have asked her for a date while he was visiting Crooked Oak.

The next time he'd seen her was at her and Lowell's wedding—and he had envied his best friend. Not that he'd wanted to get caught in the marriage trap—he certainly wasn't the marrying kind. And not that he wanted to trade lives with Lowell. He had only wanted happiness for Lowell and his new bride.

The minister ended the graveside service with a prayer. The rain grew heavier and more intense as the wind increased, blowing the moisture inside the canopy enclosure. He watched as his sister Tallie helped Susan to her feet and Caleb's wife, Sheila, held an umbrella over her as they led her toward the governor's limousine.

Grateful that Susan wasn't alone—that his family had

rallied around her—Hank stayed at the graveside until the crowd cleared. The attendants from the funeral home waited while he stood over Lowell's casket, placed his hand on the cold, damp metal and made a silent vow. *I promise you that I'll take care of Susan and the baby.*

As he walked away, he felt a hand on his shoulder. Glancing back, he saw his younger brother Caleb.

"Are you all right?" Caleb asked.

"Yeah."

The two men walked side by side toward Hank's rental car. The rain soaked them, plastering their hair to their heads.

"I'll ride with you," Caleb said. "I think Peyt's limo is full, with Peyt and Tallie, as well as Donna and Sheila in there with Susan."

The brothers got into the Taurus and sat silently for several minutes before the cars in front of them began to move. Hank shifted into drive and followed the procession out of the cemetery.

"Never thought the sheriff of a quiet little hick county like ours would wind up getting himself murdered." Caleb shook his head.

"Yeah, you're right. There's not much crime around here, is there? Lowell wasn't the type who sought out danger or wanted anything more than to keep the peace."

"Ole Lowell always reminded me of TV's Andy Taylor without Barney." Caleb chuckled. "God, he was a good man!"

"The best." Hank felt a knot of emotion tighten in his chest. He had cared for Lowell Redman the way he cared about Caleb and Jake, as if he'd been another brother. They'd been friends since first grade. Hank had always been the leader, the instigator, the one daring Lowell to take risks with him. And Lowell had been the faithful follower, the accessory to their boyish pranks, the quiet, bash-ful boy who didn't have an adventurous bone in his body.

"I hope they find the son of a bitch who shot him," Caleb said. "Damn dopehead! That Carl Bates has always been a worthless piece of trash."

"Bates can't run and hide forever," Hank said. "Usually guys like him wind up coming home and looking for help. We'll get him. You can bet on that."

Within minutes Hank pulled the Taurus up outside Su-san's house, but didn't kill the motor.

Caleb turned to him. "Aren't you coming in? Susan will expect you to be there. Half the town will come through those doors before nightfall. I know it would mean a lot to her if Lowell's best friend was at her side."

The last thing Susan probably wanted was for him to be at her side all evening, while friends and acquaintances paraded in and out to pay their condolences. She had to be as numb as he over losing Lowell and as stunned and un-certain as he about her pregnancy. But the odd thing was, he really wanted to be there with her. She had looked so fragile, so vulnerable, during the funeral. Small-boned and slender, Susan came just to his shoulder. More than once since he'd seen her last night, he had wanted to lift her into his arms, take her away from the endless horde of people trying to console her and keep her safely under his protec-tion.

Hank killed the motor. "You're right. I need to be with Susan."

Her entire body was as numb as her emotions. She'd been on display for hours last night and then again today at the funeral and the graveside service. Tallie and Sheila had suggested that she lie down for a while, but Donna had been the one who had fended them off when she'd insisted on staying to meet every person who came by to share her grief. Donna was a widow herself, having lost her husband over five years ago, and she was the only one of her close friends who understood exactly what she was going through today. The last thing Susan needed right now was to be alone, lying down in the quiet, dark bedroom she had shared with Lowell.

Susan saw him the minute he entered the room. Tall, whipcord lean, with shoulders that looked five feet wide in his tan trench coat. His jet-black hair was damp, one strand curling down over his forehead. Hank Bishop. Her husband's oldest and dearest friend. The man who had been best man at her wedding. The man she'd had a secret crush on during her teen years. The man she had fantasized about more than once when Lowell made love to her.

She shivered as guilt washed over her. She had no right to think of Hank Bishop in that way. No right whatsoever. She had loved Lowell. Who wouldn't have? Lowell Redman had been the kindest, most gentle and loving man she'd ever known. And he had given her a good, safe and secure life as his wife. She'd been past thirty when they'd married, well past the age of expecting Prince Charming to come along and sweep her off her feet. Besides, she knew herself well enough to know that anyone daring enough to sweep her off her feet would frighten her to death. Susan wasn't a risk taker when it came to men and to life in general.

Lowell had been safe. Hank Bishop wasn't.

Hank was dangerous to her. He always had been and he always would be. Just because in her secret fantasies she dreamed of being ravaged and claimed by Hank, didn't mean she had actually wanted the man in her life.

He was walking toward her, his dark eyes seeking her out from the crowd. Her stomach quivered. Her heart fluttered. She wanted to scream at him, tell him to go away and never come back. She couldn't bear to have him so close to her. She was afraid of leaning on him. More than anything she wanted his strong arms around her, wanted him to promise that he would take care of her and make everything all right. But no one, not even Hank, could make things right again. Her safe and secure life had been utterly and completely destroyed. The future with Lowell as her husband and father of her child had vanished like smoke in the wind. Somehow she had to find the strength to raise this child alone—this sweet little baby that Lowell had wanted so desperately.

The same moment Susan laid her hand over her abdomen in a protective gesture, she noticed Hank watching her more intently, his gaze moving downward from her face to her hand. The look in his eyes frightened her. Protective. Possessive. Predatory.

"There's Hank," Sheila said, slipping her arm around Susan's waist. "Maybe he can persuade you to eat a bite and then get some rest."

"I told you that I'm fine," Susan said. "I wish you and Tallie would stop hovering about as if you think I might pass out at any minute."

Leaning over, Sheila whispered in Susan's ear, "Does Hank know you're pregnant?"

Susan nodded solemnly. Biting down on her lip, she forced herself to stay calm, not to lash out at her friend for being concerned. "I told him last night at the funeral home."

"Good. He should know the situation."

"Who should know what situation?" Caleb asked as he and Hank approached.

Susan felt heat suffuse her face and prayed no one would notice, or that if they did, they wouldn't guess the reason.

"Hank." She cleared her throat. "Hank, you should know that you're probably going to be offered Lowell's job. Several people have already mentioned that they'd like to see you come home and take over the investigation into Lowell's murder.''

''They want me to be sheriff?'' Hank asked.

''Yeah,'' Caleb said. ''Some of the commissioners mentioned to me that they'd like to have you appointed to finish out Lowell's term so you could bring his killer to justice. There's about a year left on his current term. They're hoping you can take a leave of absence from the Bureau.''

''But I don't—''

''If you accepted the appointment, you'd be around to help look after Susan and—'' Sheila said, stopping abruptly when Susan jabbed her in the ribs with her elbow.

''I don't need anyone to look after me!'' Susan realized too late that not only had she spoken sharply, but she'd practically shouted her comment. Several people within earshot turned their heads and glanced in her direction.

Afraid he would see the fear in her eyes, she looked everywhere but at Hank. ''I'm sorry,'' she told them. ''I suppose I am tired. Maybe Sheila's right. Perhaps I should go lie down for a while.''

She moved past Hank quickly, not sparing him even a glance. What would she do if he stayed on in Crooked Oak? He wouldn't do that, would he? He couldn't!

''Susan's not herself,'' Sheila said by way of explanation to the onlookers. ''Y'all must know what losing Lowell has done to her.''

People nodded in agreement and quickly began talking among themselves. Commissioner Kelly threw up a hand in greeting, then waved at Hank, motioning him to join his circle.

''Here it comes,'' Caleb said. ''Get ready to be offered Lowell's old job.''

''I can't take Lowell's job!'' *And I can't take on his wife and child.* ''I don't want to be sheriff of Marshall County.''

''Then you're going to have to tell them that.'' Caleb

patted his brother on the back. "But I must admit that I'm surprised you aren't willing to take a leave of absence and come back home long enough to put things right for Lowell. He left an unfinished job and a pregnant wife who's going to need someone to lean on."

"I didn't realize you knew Susan was pregnant," Hank said.

"Sheila told me this morning. But how did you know?"

"Susan told me last night at the funeral home."

"See, she told you because she knows she's going to need you. She's going to need all of us to get through these next few months. Knowing you, I figured you'd think you owed it to Lowell to see his killer brought to justice and to take care of his wife and child."

"I owe Lowell my life," Hank admitted. "But I'm not sure that staying here in Crooked Oak is the right way to repay him."

The brothers walked together toward Commissioner Kelly, who had been joined by two other county commissioners in a corner of the room that proudly displayed Susan's old-maid aunt's antique dining room suite. A feast, brought in by friends and neighbors, covered the mahogany table and desserts of every kind lined the ornately carved buffet. Dalton Kelly sliced off a bite of apple pie with his fork and lifted it to his mouth.

Rufus McGee shook hands with Hank. "Good to see you again, Hank. Just hate that it's under these circumstances."

After washing down the pie with a swig of black coffee, Dalton swiped his mouth with his hand, then said, "Has Caleb told you what we want to ask of you?"

"Yes, he just mentioned it," Hank said.

"And what do you think, boy?" Rufus narrowed his eyes, staring directly at Hank. "Are you willing to take a little time off from the FBI to come home and settle things for Lowell? We'd be mighty grateful if you would."

"Why me?" Hank asked. "I'd think y'all would be talking to Richard Holman about the job. I know Lowell trusted Deputy Holman completely and felt he was the best man he had working for him."

"Richard's young and doesn't have enough experience," Dalton said. "Besides, it'd only be for a year, just until next year's election. You could give up a year for Lowell, couldn't you?"

"The whole town is expecting you to come home," Rufus said. "They're sure you'll want to be the one to capture Carl Bates and bring him to justice. And they're expecting you to take care of Susan for Lowell. We know her delicate condition is suppose to be a secret, but well—" Rufus grinned "—Lowell's chest was so swelled with pride the day they found out about the baby, he was popping buttons off his shirt. He told a few friends, and you know how word spreads around these parts."

Hank's stomach knotted painfully. He'd been on assignment when word reached him of Lowell's death. When he'd checked his answering machine on a quick stop at his Alexandria apartment, he'd heard Lowell's happy voice asking him to call him as soon as possible. No doubt Lowell had wanted to tell him about the baby.

"I'll need some time," Hank said. "I'll have to go back to Washington and...I'm not sure this is the right thing to do, but—"

"It is, my boy. It is," Dalton assured him. "Just think about what Lowell would have done if you'd been murdered in the line of duty, leaving behind your killer on the loose and a pregnant wife who needed somebody to lean on. Wouldn't he have done everything he could have for you? He'd have put your killer behind bars. And he'd have taken care of your wife and baby."

Hell! He was caught dead to right. The whole town knew that not only were he and Lowell best friends, but that he owed Lowell his life. When they'd been teenagers—he thirteen and Lowell fourteen—they'd gone swimming at the old abandoned rock quarry, as they had so often that summer. But he had gotten a severe cramp and would have drowned if it hadn't been for Lowell's quick action. The event had sealed their friendship for life, and to this day, Hank felt he owed his life to his friend.

He'd do anything for Lowell. Even now. The way he saw it, he really didn't have any choice but to put his career on hold and return to Crooked Oak. Was a year of his life too much of a sacrifice to come home and settle his best friend's affairs? No, of course it wasn't. If only those affairs didn't include Lowell's pregnant wife!

Once this crowd cleared out, he'd have to talk to Susan—alone. Lowell's death had placed them in an awkward situation and the last thing he wanted was to complicate his life or cause Susan any unnecessary pain.

Susan sat on the bed in the quiet, semidark bedroom that she had shared with Lowell the past two years. She wasn't sure she'd ever be able to sleep in this room again, not unless she completely renovated it and bought all new furniture. Everything in the large, airy room reminded her of her husband. The smell of his spicy cologne still lingered on the bed linen. His clothes filled the left side of the closet. Their wedding photograph sat like a sentinel on the nightstand.

If only she could cry. *Dear Lord in heaven,* she silently pleaded, *let me cry.* But she was beyond crying, the pain too severe, yet tempered by the blessed numbness that cocooned her.

A shudder racked her body. Ricky gazed up at her with his big, black Boston terrier eyes, as if questioning her. She scratched his ears and whispered, "I'll be okay. Don't worry about me."

Seeing that his mistress was paying attention to Ricky, Fred waddled across the room, hopped up onto the bed and parked his fat little bulldog body alongside Ricky. "Oh, so you're jealous, huh?" Susan rubbed the other dog's ears, then heard a soft, subtle purring. Resting at the foot of the bed, Lucy, a red tabby, and Ethel, a white longhair, mewed for their share of attention.

A sigh of relief escaped Susan's lips. Relief that something remained normal and unchanged in her life. Her animals were now, as they had been all her life, a source of companionship and comfort. She loved animals and they her. She supposed that was another legacy from Aunt Alice—the old-maid great-aunt who had taken her in and raised her after her mother's death. She'd been six when she'd come to live with Aunt Alice in this big, old Victorian house filled with priceless antiques, several spoiled cats and one feisty Boston terrier pup, Ricky's grandmother. Susan had grown up around animals, so her job at the animal shelter was a natural career choice.

In the darkest, loneliest hours of her life, her animals were at her side. Loving her. Supporting her. Comforting her. She lifted both dogs onto her lap and hugged them tenderly. A lone tear escaped from her eye and trickled down her cheek. Then another followed. Her lungs swelled. Her chest ached. She gasped for air. Her shoulders trembled. And then the tears began in earnest. Filling her eyes. Flooding her face. Moistening her chin and neck.

Susan didn't know how long she cried, whether it was minutes or hours. No one invaded her privacy, not even when she cried aloud as sobs racked her body.

She knew that Tallie and Sheila and Donna were taking turns guarding her bedroom door against all intruders. She was a lucky woman to have such good friends. She and Tallie and Sheila had been best buddies since childhood and then Donna had joined their inner circle several years ago.

Susan lifted her head from her hands when she heard a soft rapping on the door. "Yes?"

"It's us," Sheila said. "Tallie and Donna and me. May we come in?"

"Of course." Susan wiped the moisture from her face and scooted to the edge of the bed.

Her three best friends entered the room and quickly made a semicircle around her. She offered them a tremulous smile.

"Just about everybody's gone," Tallie said.

"Hank and Caleb and Peyton are still here, of course," Sheila said.

"Are you sure you don't want me to stay with you tonight?" Tallie asked.

"No, really. I'll be all right." She glanced back at the big bed on which she sat. "I won't sleep in here. I slept upstairs last night, in Aunt Alice's old room. Being in her room comforted me. It made me feel close to her."

"I'd like to stay." Donna sat down beside Susan. "I can run home and pack a few things and stay with you for as long as you need me. Believe me, I know how difficult these next few months are going to be for you."

Susan grabbed Donna's hand and squeezed tightly. "I know you understand better than anyone. But—"

"I insist. Unlike Sheila and Tallie, I don't have a husband and children at home."

"Thank you." Susan nodded. "It would be nice to have someone here for a few days. Just until—" Susan choked on the tears in her throat. "Just until I—" The dam burst again, releasing a torrent of tears.

Donna took Susan in her arms, stroking and comforting, while Sheila and Tallie hovered nearby. The three women tried valiantly not to cry, but within minutes they, too, were weeping.

"I'll stay until you get back," Hank told Donna Fields.

"Thanks. I really don't think she should be alone." Donna patted Hank on the shoulder. "She's going to need all of her friends and Lowell's friends to see her through this."

Hank opened the door to Donna's Corvette and waited until she backed out of the driveway before he returned inside the house. Before they left, his sister and sister-in-law had cleared away the tables, packed the food in the refrigerator and freezer, loaded the dishwasher and vacuumed the floors.

A hushed stillness enveloped the house, a big gingerbread-trimmed Victorian that had been built outside of town more than ninety years ago by Susan's great-grandparents. Their youngest daughter, Alice Williams, had inherited the place, and Miss Alice, as everyone in Crooked Oak had called her, had become the local eccentric. The old-maid schoolteacher with a hundred cats.

But actually, there had been only five cats, and Miss Alice, though a unique personality, hadn't been wealthy enough to qualify for eccentric status. He had liked and admired Miss Alice, and because he'd been an excellent student, she had taken a special interest in him. She had been the first teacher who'd made him realize that he was intelligent and that by using that intelligence, he could escape the poverty of his life in Crooked Oak, Tennessee.

"Would you care for some coffee?" Susan asked.

Hank turned abruptly to face her. He hadn't realized she was standing there, in the hallway. He'd thought she was still barricaded in her bedroom.

"No, thanks," he replied.

"What about some tea? I'm going to fix myself some herbal tea."

"I don't like hot tea."

"Oh. All right then."

Damn! He suddenly realized that Susan felt as awkward as he did. The two of them alone here in her house. The house she had shared with Lowell for two years.

But they had to face facts. Lowell was dead. God, how that admission hurt him. He could not imagine a world without Lowell Redman. But no matter how much they wanted things to be different—and they both did—neither of them could undo what had happened. Not what had happened two days ago when Lowell had been ambushed by Carl Bates. And not what had happened in a doctor's office four weeks ago when Susan had been artificially inseminated.

"We need to talk," he said as he followed her into the kitchen.

"Yes, I suppose we do." She filled the teakettle with water and placed it on the stove.

"I've been asked to take over Lowell's job until next year's election."

Biting her bottom lip, Susan removed a china teacup and saucer from the cupboard, then opened a canister and retrieved a tea bag. "Are you going to accept the offer?" Her hand quivered ever so slightly as she placed the tea bag in the cup.

"Yes." Why wouldn't she turn around and face him? Would it be that big a problem for her to have him back in Crooked Oak for the next year? "I think I owe it to Lowell to bring in Carl Bates and see that he goes to trial. And I think Lowell would want me around to look after you while you're pregnant."

Tears gathered in her eyes. The teakettle whistled. As she lifted the china cup and saucer from the table, her shoulders shook and her hand trembled. The cup and saucer crashed onto the hardwood floor.

"Susan?" Hank rushed over to her, stopping her as she knelt to pick up the pieces of broken china. "Leave it. I'll clean it up."

She hummed with sorrow, crying in a low, mournful chant. God in heaven, what was he supposed to do? He wanted to touch her, but did he dare? He had to take her in his arms. He had to! She was falling apart right in front of him.

The moment he touched her, surrounding her slender body with his, taking her into his arms, Susan melted against him. Every nerve in his body screamed.

"It's all right, Susie Q," he told her, using the nickname he'd given her when she'd been a kid. "You go ahead and get it all out. I'll be here for you. I'm not going anywhere."

She clung to him. Sobbing. Trembling. Moaning. He held her as gently as he could, all his protective instincts on high and putting him on edge.

She lifted her head from his chest and looked up at him with red-rimmed eyes. "I'll be all right." She stepped out of his embrace and took a wobbly step backward. When he reached out to steady her, she moved uneasily away.

"I realize that you want to do what you can to bring Lowell's killer to justice…" She paused, took a deep breath and then continued. "If you move back to Crooked Oak—"

"When I move back to Crooked Oak," he corrected her.

"Yes. When you move back, I'm sure we'll see each other from time to time during the next year. That can't be avoided. People will expect us to…to…"

"To be friendly toward each other."

"Yes. And I want that. I want us to be friends. Lowell would have wanted us to be… If I need you, I'll call you. But I have friends who'll be here for me and, most importantly, I have my baby. Having my child to think about will see me through the rough times.''

"My child." Hank had said the words without thinking, his voice a strained whisper.

"No!" she protested. "This baby is Lowell's child."

"I realize you think of the child as Lowell's, but we both know that I fathered your baby." Hank laid his hand over her flat belly.

She froze on the spot. "The agreement was for you to donate your sperm because Lowell didn't want a stranger to father our child." Susan snatched Hank's hand off her stomach. "Lowell trusted you to keep our secret, to let this baby be his completely."

"And if Lowell had lived, I would have adhered to the terms of that agreement. But Lowell is dead. He can't be a father to your baby."

"Yes, he…Lowell is…" Tears streamed down her face.

Hank grasped her shoulders. "The child you're carrying is mine. And whether you like it or not, now that Lowell is dead, it's my responsibility to take care of you!"

Two

Lowell had been dead ten days. Ten of the worst days of her life. All their plans for the future had died with him—the happy family life that they had envisioned when their baby was born. But Lowell would never see their child—the child he had so desperately wanted. A child that he had known she wanted more than anything on earth.

When the doctors told them that it was unlikely, if not impossible, that Lowell would ever impregnate her, he had been the one to embrace the idea of artificial insemination. She had been reluctant at the thought of a stranger fathering her child, but she'd become even more reluctant when Lowell had suggested asking Hank Bishop to donate his sperm.

"Hank's said more than once that he's not the marrying kind," Lowell had told her. "He doesn't want a wife and kids."

"What makes you think Hank would agree to—to donate his sperm so that we can have a baby?"

"Because Hank thinks he owes me for saving his life when we were kids. Besides, he's the only man I know I'd want to be the biological father of our child. Hank's smart, a real man's man and the best friend I've ever had."

At first she had refused to even consider Hank as the donor, but eventually Lowell had worn down her resistance. *Lowell and your own foolish girlhood dreams!* an inner voice taunted.

"Need any help in here, Mrs. Redman?" Deputy Nancy Steele asked as she poked her head inside the door.

"No, thanks, Nancy. I've got just about everything packed away."

"Well, when you're ready to put the boxes in your van, let me know and some of us will take them out for you."

"All right. Thank you."

"Sure thing."

"Oh, Nancy?"

"Yes?"

"I'd like to leave a message for Hank Bishop."

"Certainly. We're expecting him sometime this afternoon," Nancy replied. "Do you want to leave a written message or a—"

"Verbal. Please tell Hank that I wish him well and that I appreciate—" Susan's voice cracked. She appreciated what? That he was going to be in Crooked Oak for the next year? That he had promised her quite vehemently that he was going to be around to look after her and the baby? His baby! He'd let her know in no uncertain terms that, with Lowell dead, he intended to take over Lowell's responsibilities for her and the child.

"I understand, Mrs. Redman." Nancy looked at Susan with pity in her eyes. "But I'm sure Mr. Bishop...er, Sheriff Bishop will be stopping by your house to check on you."

Dear God, that's what I'm afraid of, Susan thought. No

one knows that this child I'm carrying isn't Lowell's biological child—no one except the doctors in Nashville, Hank Bishop and Sheila. Would the townspeople believe Hank's attention to her was nothing more than a good friend looking out for his buddy's widow?

"Yes, I'm sure you're right. After all, Hank was Lowell's oldest and dearest friend. It would be only natural that he'd keep an eye on me, especially…"

"We're all so sorry about Lowell. He was the best man I ever knew. But you have his child and that should be a comfort to you."

"Yes, it is." Susan almost choked on the lie. *But this isn't Lowell's baby,* she wanted to scream. *Don't you see, that's the problem?*

"I'll go so you can finish up in here. Let me know when you're ready to leave." Nancy exited the office and closed the door behind her.

Susan sat in Lowell's big, swivel desk chair and glanced around his office. No, not Lowell's office any longer. Not after today. Appointed by the governor, Hank Bishop would be sworn in as the new Marshall County sheriff tomorrow morning.

She should have cleared out Lowell's things days ago, but somehow she hadn't been able to bring herself to face the task. To clean out his desk, to remove his certificates and pictures from the walls, to remove his books and magazines from the small bookshelf in the corner.

She lifted the silver frame that lay atop one of the open boxes on the desk. A smiling couple looked back at her from the photograph. Her wedding picture. Lowell and she had been very happy that day, the first day of their married life together. Lowell had loved her deeply and had been completely devoted to her. He'd been the kindest, most considerate lover, and her wedding night had been a prelude to many nights of gentle lovemaking.

Susan caressed Lowell's image with her fingertips. "Oh, you sweet, sweet man. What am I going to do without you? You were my protector. My shield against the world. You kept me safe and secure. As long as I had you, I didn't have to be afraid of…"

She couldn't say it out loud. Couldn't voice her greatest fear. But the secret she'd kept buried in her heart for so long could no longer be ignored. Lowell couldn't save her from herself anymore. He couldn't save her from the wild, illogical passion she'd always felt for Hank Bishop.

She clutched the picture frame in her hands, laid her forehead on the glass and wept.

A few minutes later Hank Bishop found her weeping when he opened the door to Lowell's office. He'd gotten an early start this morning and arrived in Crooked Oak before noon. When Deputy Steele told him that Susan was clearing out Lowell's office, he walked right in, hoping to offer his help.

He stood in the doorway and watched her as she cried. He wanted to go over and take her into his arms. Dammit, why was it that Susan Williams Redman was the only woman on earth who affected him this way? He had always liked the ladies, although he'd never been a ladies' man like his brothers Caleb and Jake. And the ladies liked him. They had often commented on his gentlemanly treatment of them before, during and after an affair. But only his best friend's widow brought forth all the possessive, protective, caring instincts within him.

It's because she's carrying your child.

Damn! He'd been a fool to agree to Lowell's request. But he had owed Lowell. And when he'd agreed to donate his sperm for the artificial insemination, he'd never considered the possibility that Lowell wouldn't be around to be a father to the child.

Lowell would have made any kid a great dad. The best

father in the world. Unlike himself, Lowell had been raised in a normal, middle-class family and had inherited his own father's wonderful parenting instincts. He, on the other hand, would make a lousy father. As lousy as his own had been before he died.

Hank had always known he wasn't cut out to be a husband and father.

So, how the hell was he going to handle being a father to the child Susan was carrying? Taking responsibility for that child was the last thing he wanted—but take responsibility he would. Hank Bishop didn't shrug off his obligations—he never had and he never would.

"Is there anything I can do to help you?" he asked, his voice low and calm.

She jerked her head up and glared at him. "Hank!"

"Sorry. I didn't mean to startle you."

"I didn't think you'd be getting in until this afternoon." Standing on shaky legs, she smoothed the wrinkles out of her skirt and nervously eyed Hank. "I was trying to get everything cleared out before you got here."

"There's no rush about that," he said, glancing at the three filled boxes on the desk. "Looks like you're about finished."

"Yes, I am. I was just about to start putting things in my minivan."

The moment Susan lifted one of the boxes, Hank rushed forward and took it away from her. Gasping, she stared at him with wide, surprised eyes.

"You shouldn't be lifting anything heavy, should you?" He glanced meaningfully at her still flat stomach. "I mean, since you're pregnant."

Instinctively she laid her hand over her belly. "The boxes aren't that heavy."

"It doesn't matter," he told her. "I'll take them out to your van for you."

"Thanks. I really should be going." She glanced around the room. "Being here in Lowell's office makes me sad. Just thinking about the fact that he'll never—" She choked back a sob.

"Yeah, I know." Carrying the box under his arm, Hank opened the door and stood back, waiting for Susan to exit. "I promise you that we'll bring Carl Bates in to see that he stands trial for what he did."

Susan walked past Hank, accelerating her steps so that she wouldn't be near him any longer than necessary. He followed her out to her Dodge Caravan, lowered the back hatch and loaded the box inside.

"I'll get the other two boxes," he said. "You go ahead and get inside out of the cold."

She nodded, got in the van and waited. When Hank had the other two boxes of Lowell's belongings loaded, he knocked on the window. Susan lowered the window and looked directly at him.

"Yes?"

"I'll follow you home and help you store Lowell's things."

"That isn't necessary, I'll—"

"We need to talk, Susan." He scanned the sidewalk, noting that several passersby had slowed their gaits and were staring at Susan and him. He nodded and smiled and the onlookers returned his smile. "We need to talk, privately."

"Yes, I suppose you're right."

He slid behind the wheel of his Lexus, backed out of the parking place and followed Susan's silver-gray Caravan down Main Street and onto the highway leading out of town.

He had thought long and hard about what he wanted to say to Susan—what he had to say to her. He just hoped she would listen to reason and accept the help he intended to offer her. No one in this town ever needed to know that the baby was his, but he had every intention of making sure his son or daughter was well taken care of. After he fulfilled Lowell's term as sheriff, he planned to return to the Bureau and resume his career. But he could be a godfather to his child, even if he had to do it long distance most of the time. He'd visit Crooked Oak occasionally, and when the child grew older, he or she could stay with him in Alexandria from time to time.

Hank pulled into the driveway directly behind Susan, got out and helped her from the van. "Why don't you go on inside? I'll get the boxes."

"I'm going to store most of the things in the basement," she said. "I've already cleared off a shelf down there."

Ten minutes later, Hank came up from the basement and found Susan in the kitchen. She had remained upstairs while he stored Lowell's things. He suspected that she couldn't bear to see those items banished into storage. The only thing she had removed from the boxes before he'd taken them to the basement was the wedding picture Lowell had kept on his desk.

Hank remembered that day. A beautiful autumn day. A simple church wedding with friends and family. A deliriously happy groom. A lovely, shy bride. And a best man who had thought, more than once, about kidnapping that innocent bride.

"I've made coffee. I'm afraid it's decaf," Susan said. "You take yours black, don't you? No sugar."

"Yeah, that's right. Thanks." He pulled out a chair at the kitchen table and sat, waiting while she poured the coffee into a bright red ceramic mug.

She poured herself a cup, added sugar and then sat across from Hank. "Thank you for putting away the boxes for me. I wonder if you would do something else for me while you're here?"

"Anything. Just ask."

"Lowell's clothes." She sucked in a deep breath. "I don't think I can bear to—"

"I'll do it. Just tell me what you want done with them."

"The homeless shelter in Marshallton can use them." She sipped the hot coffee.

"I'll take them over there myself."

"I don't know what to do with his uniforms." She surveyed Hank's big body. "They're too small for you."

"Do you want me to take them with me, too?"

"Yes. Everything. Please. Even his underwear and socks and… Lowell would have wanted them to go to someone who could use them."

"Lowell was a kindhearted man."

"I was very lucky to have him for my husband." *I wanted you,* she wanted to tell him, *not Lowell. But I was too afraid of you to ever pursue you. I knew instinctively that I wasn't strong enough for a man like you, that you'd devour me whole. I settled for a safer, tamer man. A man who worshiped the ground I walked on. You never would have loved me the way Lowell did. And I couldn't wait forever for another Prince Charming.*

"He told me more than once how lucky he was that you had married him." Hank laid his hands flat on the table, palms down. *And every time he told me how wonderful you were, I wanted you all the more.*

"I loved him," Susan said, her voice soft and low.

"I'm sure you did. And you must know how much he loved you."

"I tried to be a good wife to him."

"You were."

"He wanted to be a perfect husband," she said. "It almost killed him when the doctors told us that he could never…that he was sterile."

"He wanted to give you a child. That's why he came to me."

Susan lifted her head and looked Hank directly in the eye. "You aren't going to tell anyone that my baby isn't Lowell's, are you?"

"You don't want anyone to know the child is mine, do you?"

She shook her head. "No. What would people around here think if they knew? As Lowell's friend, you and I can have a friendly relationship and you can be my child's favorite Uncle Hank. But if people knew you were my baby's father, they'd watch us and judge us and—"

"I'm going to tell Caleb," he said. "No one else."

"Promise?"

It took a great deal of strength not to reach across the table and grab her small, delicate hands, but Hank resisted the almost overwhelming urge.

"Susan, why are you so afraid of me? Don't you know that I'd never hurt you?" Every time she looked at him, he saw the fear in her eyes. Was there something more to her fear than not wanting anyone to know the truth about their child? If so, what was it?

"But you could hurt me," she said, gazing into her lap, letting her long lashes shade her eyes. "If you don't keep my secret…our secret. Yours and mine and Lowell's."

"I want to tell my brother, but I promise no one else will know."

Susan gulped in a large swallow of air and nodded her head affirmatively. "All right. Tell Caleb. Sheila has been my one confidante, so…"

"This isn't what I wanted, either." Hank shoved the untouched mug of coffee away from him, scooted back his chair and stood. "I never planned on being a father. The last thing I need in my life is a child. The plan was for that baby—'' he glanced at her stomach ''—to be Lowell's and yours. Not mine.''

''I haven't asked you to take responsibility for this child,'' she told him, her cheeks flushed with emotion. ''I don't expect you to be a father to—''

Hank slammed his fist into the palm of his hand, creating a loud smack. Susan jumped.

''Dammit, don't you see? Without Lowell around, that kid isn't going to have a father unless I step in and do the right thing.''

''And just what is the 'right thing,' Hank?'' She watched him pace the floor in her kitchen, his big, lean body stalking back and forth like an animal trying to escape a captor's trap. And that had to be the way he saw her and her baby— a threat to his much-loved freedom.

''I don't know.''

Yes, you do, some inner voice urged.

The right thing to do would be to marry Susan and for the two of them to raise their child in a family unit. But heaven help him, he wasn't willing to put his head in that particular noose—no matter how desirable he found Susan or how determined he was to not abandon his child.

''The right thing is for me to do what I can to take care of you while you're pregnant and then to take financial responsibility for my child.''

''I see.'' Susan eased back her chair, stood and faced Hank. ''You've undoubtedly given this a great deal of thought.''

''Look at it from a logical standpoint. You're a pregnant widow, without parents or brothers and sisters to help you. As Lowell's best friend, no one is going to think it odd that I've elected myself as your guardian or the child's godfather.''

''Yes, you're right, of course. And I know I should be

grateful that you're willing to give up a year of your life, to take a leave of absence from the FBI and—''

"I don't want your gratitude," he told her. "I want your cooperation."

He infuriated her with his cool logic. So calm and controlled. So unemotional. She was sure he hadn't shed one single tear for Lowell. Hank wasn't the kind of man who cried. Not ever. No matter how much he was suffering.

Tallie had told her once that of her three brothers, Hank was the most bitter and resentful about having been raised poor and parentless. Where Tallie had no memory of their parents and Caleb only vague memories, Hank and Jake did remember. Their father had been a gambler and a drinker and they'd moved from pillar to post and had often been run out of town by the local authorities. When their parents had been killed in an accident, the four Bishop children had come to Crooked Oak to live with their paternal grandfather, a good man but not a warm and loving parent by any stretch of the imagination.

"Hank won't ever marry and have kids," Tallie had told her. "He'll never take the chance that he might not be as perfect at fatherhood as he is at everything else."

Remembering her friend's words, Susan sighed. "All right, Hank. I'll cooperate." She held out her hand, pretending that she was as unemotional and in control of the situation as he was. "You'll watch over me until the baby's born and then you'll be his or her godfather, doting 'Uncle Hank.' But no one, other than Sheila and Caleb, will ever know Lowell isn't the father of my child."

The thing Hank wanted most at that very minute was to touch Susan, to take her hand and pull her close. And it was the last thing on earth he should do. He stared at her proffered hand—a gesture to seal the bargain.

She waited, shifting uncomfortably several times before he reached out and took her hand in his. The moment his skin touched hers, she felt an electrical current zing through her body. She closed her eyes momentarily and prayed for the strength to not succumb to the desire she felt for this man. How could she be so wanton? Lowell hadn't been dead two weeks!

Hank held her hand and gazed into her big blue eyes. He should be damned to hell for what he was thinking—for what he was feeling. If he acted on his desire, he'd scare her to death and offend her so grievously that she'd never forgive him.

He shook her hand, then released it and stepped away from her. "I'll come back over tonight and pack up Lowell's clothes."

"All right. Thank you."

"If you need me, I'll be in the sheriff's office this afternoon, and later, I'll be out at Caleb and Sheila's. I'm staying with them temporarily, until I find a place to live."

"I'll see you to the door."

When he turned around, she followed him. He didn't pause until he stepped out on the front porch, then he faced her briefly, smiled weakly and nodded farewell. She stood in the open doorway and watched him as he drove off down the road.

Tears trickled from the corners of her eyes, dampening her cheeks in their descent. Life was unfair. So terribly unfair. She'd taken every precaution to keep her unrequited love for Hank Bishop from becoming an obsession. She had loved him from afar when she'd been a teenager, mooned over him the way some girls mooned over rock stars. But he had never noticed her, except as Tallie's little friend, and deep within her she had known it was for the best. As much as she adored Hank, she was afraid of the way he made her feel.

Aunt Alice had insisted she always be the perfect little lady. No vulgar displays. No immoral thoughts or feelings.

"Sex" was an unspoken word—a strictly taboo subject in her aunt's house. What she felt for Hank had been wrong, and probably sinful, and had certainly frightened her. So, she had dated the safe boys—the ones who didn't make butterflies soar in her stomach or create tingling sensations in the most intimate parts of her body.

Hank had left Crooked Oak and she had prayed for Prince Charming to come along and sweep her off her feet, to make her fall in love with him and give her a happily-ever-after life. And she had been sure that she wouldn't feel ashamed of or frightened by the way Prince Charming made her feel.

At thirty, she'd given up hope of this sweet and safe Prince Charming and settled for sweet and safe Lowell Redman. She had loved Lowell. And her feelings for him had never scared her, never frightened her, never consumed her to the point of madness.

No, those emotions had been reserved for Hank Bishop. The man whose child was now growing inside her body.

Three

"That's the last box," Hank said as he closed the car trunk. "I'll take these things over to the shelter in Marshallton tomorrow."

Susan stood on the front porch, the last rays of sunlight streaking her light brown hair with gold. She looked so small and fragile and alone, like a drifting soul seeking a safe haven. He wanted to open his arms and tell her to come to him—that she could find sanctuary there, within the boundaries of his protection. He could offer, but would she accept?

He hesitated by the car, watching her as she waited for him, her head bowed and her eyes downcast. Two cats curled about her legs and two fat little dogs stood guard on either side of her. Sweet Susan, with a heart as big as all outdoors. He'd never known anyone who loved animals the way she did. And every critter on earth took to her as if she were one of them.

How was he going to be around this woman—this kind, gentle, loving woman—let alone take care of her for the next year, without making love to her?

Women came and went in his life. He had deliberately steered clear of long-term relationships and women who would expect more of him than he was willing to give. He liked women—hell, he loved women. And they seemed to not only like him, but to be drawn to him. Jake had once told him that the fairer sex was attracted to Caleb because he was so damn pretty and later because he was a superstar athlete. And they were attracted to Hank because he was such an old-fashioned, Southern gentleman, with a hint of danger to pique their interest.

Susan Redman was different. She was absolutely nothing like the women he had dated. She was quiet and shy and a little naive. And she made him want her in a way that shook him badly. He was a man who took pride in always being in control of his actions and his emotions. But his attraction to Susan undermined his iron will.

"Is there anything else I can help you with today?" he asked, not wanting to leave. Not yet.

She lifted her head and focused her gaze on him. Even at a distance, he could see the sheen of tears misting her eyes. *God, honey, don't cry,* he wanted to tell her. *Lowell wouldn't have wanted you to be in so much pain. And I can't bear seeing you like this.*

"No. There's nothing else to be done. Not today." She smiled weakly and the sight of her sad little face unnerved him.

"Well, then, I guess I'll go." *Don't let me leave,* he silently pleaded. *Ask me to stay. Think of a reason to keep me here.* He turned his back to her.

"Wait!" She took several hesitant steps forward, then halted at the edge of the porch.

He snapped his head around and walked up the brick walkway. "What is it?"

"I—I need to talk to you." She held her hands together in front of her, as if she had to restrain herself from reaching out for him.

"Sure." He walked up the steps and stopped directly in front of her, only a couple of feet separating them. "What do you want to talk to me about?"

His gaze followed hers as she glanced around, noticing that Mrs. Dobson, whose house was across the street, was thoroughly cleaning the glass in her front door and that Mrs. Brown, whose house was on Susan's right, was sweeping her porch. Small towns were full of curious people and busybodies who couldn't keep their noses out of other people's business. No doubt both Mrs. Brown and Mrs. Dobson would take note of his presence and report to their friends and neighbors. Personally, he didn't give a damn what people thought or what they said, but he knew Susan probably cared. After all, she had to live and work in Crooked Oak and would be raising her child here.

"Let's go inside." She eased backward and opened the front door.

Hank followed her, but before he stepped inside the foyer, he turned and waved at Mrs. Dobson across the street. She waved back and smiled.

Then he called out, "How are you, Mrs. Brown?"

The gray-haired woman blushed, but smiled warmly. "Just fine, Hank. Good to see you're looking after our Susan."

Hank waved. "You'll be seeing a lot of me around here."

"Glad to hear it," Mrs. Brown said.

Hank entered the foyer where Susan waited, hands in front of her, head bowed and eyes glancing up shyly.

"They've been hovering over me like mother hens ever since Lowell died. They're nosy, but their hearts are in the right place."

"Yeah, I know. I grew up in this town, remember?"

"Close the door, please."

He did as she asked. "You wanted to talk to me about something?"

She rubbed her hands together repeatedly. "While you're here in Crooked Oak, finishing up Lowell's term as sheriff, you're going to need a place to stay."

"That's right." What was she getting at? What was she trying to say. "I'm going to contact a Realtor tomorrow. Sheila's told me that I'm welcome to stay with them as long as I'd like, but I really need a place of my own."

She looked at him uncertainly. "Hank, I—I…"

She turned from him. Her small shoulders trembled. With his heartbeat pounding in his ears, he closed the distance between them and wrapped his arms around her. Shivering uncontrollably, she breathed in a gasping sob.

"You're not alone, Susan," he whispered as he lowered his lips to her ear. "I know how difficult it's going to be for you without Lowell, but I promise I'm going to be here for you during your pregnancy. I want to help make things as easy for you as possible."

She nodded. "I know."

He held her with gentle firmness and willed his body not to respond to the small, slender woman in his embrace. "We both loved Lowell and we're both going to miss him. I intend to do all I can to set things right for him. And that includes making sure his wife doesn't want for anything."

"I need you to promise me that you won't tell anyone about your being…about Lowell not being… People wouldn't understand."

"I thought I'd made it perfectly clear that I'm not going to tell anybody anything."

He kissed the side of her forehead, then rubbed his cheek against hers. Her hair smelled like sunshine and flowers. His body tightened. Loosening his hold around her, he stepped back. The last thing Susan needed was to feel his arousal pressing against her. He grasped her shoulders and slowly turned her to face him.

"I want to help you, to make things easier for you, not more difficult. There's no need for anyone to know about our personal business."

She breathed deeply. The trembling in her body subsided and she smiled at Hank. "We have to remember that your stay in Crooked Oak is only temporary. You have a job and a life somewhere else and I have a life here. Our only connection is my child." She reached up and laid her hands on his chest, against the smooth, cool fabric of his overcoat. "I know that with Lowell dead, you feel a responsibility for my baby, but I realize that I shouldn't expect you to be a father to this child. Lowell told me that you didn't want children of your own and you didn't intend to ever marry."

"I don't intend to marry and I don't want children." Hank ran his hands up and down her arms, caressing her tenderly. "But you're right. I do feel a great deal of responsibility for your baby." He released her abruptly. "I never considered this possibility when Lowell asked me to donate my sperm so you and he could have a child."

"I'm sorry, Hank." She touched his arm.

Don't touch me, he wanted to shout. *And don't look at me with those big blue eyes that ask for so much.* "Yeah, I'm sorry, too. Fate has played a pretty nasty trick on us and we're going to have to deal with it."

"I'd like to be able to tell you that I don't need you, but that would be a lie. I do need you. I need you for the next few months. If you could…if you would—"

"You name it and you've got it. I'll do whatever you need for me to do."

"Be my friend. Be an uncle—a godfather—to my baby."

"Sure. All right. Anything else?"

"Find Lowell's murderer and bring him to justice."

"That's my number one priority as sheriff."

"Be careful, Hank." She squeezed his arm. "I don't think I could bear it if anything happened to you, too."

Her words hit him like a sledgehammer blow to his midsection. He'd have to be a blind fool not to realize that Susan cared about him. But was that caring anything more than concern for Lowell's best friend? Concern for the biological father of her baby?

She sat in the quiet stillness of the den as twilight approached and evening shadows fell across the room. Lucy and Ethel perched on the back of the sofa. Curled on the rug in front of the fireplace, Ricky snored softly. And Fred cuddled close to Susan's side.

She needed to put her life back on track, to find a way to go on without Lowell. For her child's sake and for the sake of her own sanity. She needed to get back to work. With only Scooter Bellamy, her assistant, as a full-time employee, the animal shelter was sorely understaffed. Being with the animals, caring for them and trying to find homes for them could fill the hours as nothing else could. The less she thought about herself and her situation, the better off she'd be.

Hank Bishop was going to be a part of her life for the next year. She might as well accept that fact and make the best of it. Whether she liked it or not, she did need Hank. She wasn't the kind of woman who wanted to go through eight more months of pregnancy alone, so who better to stand by her than the father of her child.

She supposed she should feel guilty for thinking of the child as Hank's instead of Lowell's. But the truth be known, she had always thought of the baby as Hank's. God forgive her.

And God forgive her for not having the courage to face her feelings for Hank before she'd married Lowell. If she'd been a different kind of woman, she would have pursued Hank, done everything in her power to ensnare him, to make him fall in love with her. But the passionate feelings that Hank had always aroused in her frightened her far more than the prospect of living her life alone. Lowell had been a compromise—love, marriage and a family with a safe man, a man whose gentle love protected her from Hank Bishop.

But Lowell was gone now and nothing stood between her and her feelings for Hank. Nothing except her own fear.

Overcome that fear, she told herself. Take an uncertain, perhaps dangerous step. You're still madly in love with Hank Bishop—and the thought of giving in to those wild, uncontrollable feelings scares you to death. Even if you get hurt, even if he leaves you, wouldn't it be better to have known what it was like to belong to Hank, if only for a short period of time, than to die not knowing?

She reached over and picked up the telephone. Fred grunted, readjusted his fat little body and buried his nose against Susan's leg. After taking a deep breath, she dialed the number.

"Hello?" Sheila Bishop said.

"Sheila, this is Susan. Is Hank there?"

"Yes, he is. We just finished dinner a few minutes ago. Do you want to talk to him?"

"Yes, please."

"Is everything all right?" Sheila asked. "You sound kind of funny."

"Everything's fine. I just need to talk to Hank."

"Okay."

Susan waited, her heart thundering, her palms damp with

perspiration, her mouth dry. What if she was making a mistake? What if she lived to regret taking such a bold step?

Stop second guessing yourself. For once in your meek little life, go for the gold.

After all, what did she have to lose in the long run? Oh, nothing but her self-respect and her heart.

"Hello?" Hank said.

"Hank, it's Susan. I found you a place to live."

"You have?"

"Yes."

"Where?"

"In the apartment over my garage." She held her breath, waiting for his reaction.

"I thought someone was living there already."

"No. It's empty. The young woman who lived there got married last month and moved out. I just haven't had a chance to do anything about renting it again."

"Are you sure about this?" He chuckled softly. "You don't think the neighbors would talk, do you?"

She laughed. "The entire population of Crooked Oak is praising you for coming home to tie up the loose ends of Lowell's life. I don't think anyone will be surprised if you move close by so you can look after your best friend's pregnant widow. That *is* what you said you wanted to do, isn't it?"

"Yes, Susan, I want to look after you…for Lowell."

"Then you'll take the apartment?"

"Sure. Why not? It will make things convenient. I'd be right there, just next door, whenever you need me. How soon do you want me to move in?"

"How about tomorrow? The place is furnished, so just bring your suitcase and whatever else you brought from your Virginia apartment."

"We can discuss rent and—"

"The rent's free," she said.

"I can't accept the place rent-free."

"Then you can earn it by doing husbandly things around the place for me." She realized too late just what she'd said. A warm flush spread up her neck and heated her face.

"I suppose you mean things like mowing the lawn and cleaning the storm windows and—"

"Yes, of course that's what I mean."

"I'll see you tomorrow evening." He paused momentarily and then said, "How about going out to dinner tomorrow night? We could drive over to Marshallton."

"How about my cooking dinner for us here?"

"I'll stop by for dinner first and then you can show me the apartment. Will six o'clock be okay?"

"Yes. Six will be fine."

Susan made her way up the wooden stairs that led to the rooms above the garage. One by one, she closed the windows she had opened early this morning to air out the place, and quickly turned on the wall heaters. She breathed in deeply and smiled. The place smelled fresh and clean. She had swept, mopped, vacuumed and dusted this morning before she'd driven to Marshallton for her first doctor's appointment.

Carrying the bed linen, she entered the bedroom, then dropped the quilts and spread on top of the dresser and tossed the bottom sheet onto the bed. When she finished making the bed, she stood back and inspected her handiwork. This was going to be Hank's bedroom for the next year, only a stone's throw away from her. He was going to sleep in that bed every night—so close and yet so far away.

She could picture Hank in this room, in this bed. Did he sleep in his underwear? In pajamas? In the nude? The thought of Hank lying naked across the bed sent shivers through Susan's body. He was tall and muscular, a big man, yet lean in his hips and belly. She could remember how he'd looked as a teenager wearing nothing but a pair of cut-off jeans when he'd washed his old car or mowed the lawn. Even then his body had been breathtakingly gorgeous. How many times had she stared at him so long and hard that Sheila and Tallie had dragged her away? As she grew older, she'd hidden her obsession with Hank more easily, until by the time he got out of college, she'd been able to see him and talk to him without showing the least sign of interest.

Aunt Alice had warned her that men like Hank Bishop weren't the marrying kind. That smart, good-looking, ambitious boys like Hank were the love-'em-and-leave-'em type. And Aunt Alice had known from personal experience. She'd given her heart to such a man and he'd given it back to her in broken pieces.

"Don't trust passion, Susan," Alice Williams had said. "When a man makes you want him so badly that you'd sell your soul to be with him, stay away from him. He's dangerous. He'll wind up breaking your heart and tossing you aside like yesterday's trash."

She had fought her feelings for Hank Bishop for as long as she could remember. She'd shied away from him, knowing her aunt had been right. Even if she could've made Hank notice her, even want her, he never could have offered her the life she wanted—marriage, children and happily-ever-after contentment. With Hank, she might have known passion, might have soared to the heavens in his arms, but at what price? She hadn't been willing to risk everything for an affair with Hank. Marrying Lowell had been the right thing to do—or so she'd thought.

Marrying Lowell, loving Lowell, hadn't made her forget Hank. Hadn't made her stop wanting him. Every time Lowell had made love to her, she'd wanted him to be Hank. She had cheated the dearest, kindest man in the world out of his rightful place in her heart. And she'd felt guilty the entire two years they were married. But guilt was a useless emotion. She couldn't change anything—not then and not now.

The funny thing was, Lowell would want her to be happy. And if Hank Bishop was what made her happy, then Lowell would bless their union.

What union? She wasn't married to Hank and she wasn't likely to ever be. That's the shy, meek Susan talking, she told herself. She knew she shouldn't listen to her. She was tired of listening to her. After all, she *was* carrying Hank's baby. Hank, the man she loved. The man she'd always loved. Wasn't it about time she grew a backbone and took a chance? Maybe she wasn't the most beautiful, exciting woman he'd ever known. Maybe he truly believed he didn't want to get married and have children. But she could change his mind. She could make him love her. She could…

As tears trickled down her cheeks, she wiped them away with her fingertips. She sat on the edge of the bed, laid both hands over her belly and focused on the unborn child inside her.

"If I don't have the courage to do it for myself, then I'm going to have to find the courage to do it for you, sweet baby. You deserve a father. Lowell Redman would have been a wonderful father to you. He would have been the best father in the world. But we don't have Lowell anymore. Who we have is Hank Bishop. And with my luck, you're probably a boy and you'll look just like him and everybody's going to know he's your father."

Susan jumped up off the bed, hurriedly put out clean towels, washcloths and a roll of toilet tissue in the bathroom, then ran a critical eye over the living room and small kitchenette hidden behind a folding screen. Nothing fancy. But it was neat and clean and homey. And Hank would probably hate it.

Checking her watch, she sighed with relief. She had

plenty of time to bake cornbread sticks, set the table and still take a nice, long bubble bath. Tonight would be Phase One in her scheme to capture Hank Bishop's heart.

Usually when Hank was invited to a lady's home for dinner, he took wine. But Susan was pregnant, so that ruled out liquor. Besides, if he remembered correctly, Susan had always been a teetotaler. After checking his appearance in the car mirror, he adjusted his striped tie and brushed back a lock of hair that had fallen onto his forehead.

Why the hell was he so nervous? He was acting like a teenager on a first date. This isn't a date, he reminded himself. This was only dinner with a friend.

A friend who happens to be pregnant with your child.

No matter how he tried to get away from that fact, he couldn't. Susan Redman *was* pregnant. He wished he could hold someone responsible for this mess, but he couldn't. No one was to blame for his current predicament. Not himself. Not Susan. And not even Lowell. None of them could have foreseen the future.

Hank reached across the seat, picked up the bouquet of flowers he'd bought at Crooked Oak's only florist, and opened the driver's door. The porch light shone brightly, like a welcoming beacon. The crisp autumn wind whipped around him as he stepped up to the front door.

If he could get through this dinner with Susan without giving in to his baser instincts, then there was hope that he could get through the next twelve months without ravaging his best friend's widow. He had to keep reminding himself that Susan wanted his friendship and needed his strength to lean on during her pregnancy. He owed it to Lowell to take care of Susan. And he owed it to the child—the baby his sperm and Susan's egg had created in some sterile doctor's office nearly six weeks ago.

Hank rang the doorbell. His gut instinct told him to run. Run like hell.

Susan opened the door, her two mutts flanking her. "Come on in. It's getting cold out there, isn't it? We're supposed to get another frost tonight."

He stood there staring at her, his jaw tense, his eyes wide. She was lovely. Absolutely lovely. Glowing and soft and feminine in her tailored pink corduroy skirt and matching cotton sweater. Her long mane of sun-kissed brown hair flowed down her back and across one shoulder.

"Is something wrong?" she asked.

"No. No, nothing's wrong." He stepped inside the foyer, closed the door behind him and held up the bouquet.

"For me?"

"I think Lowell once told me that your favorite flowers are lilies." Hank cleared his throat. "I remember that's what you carried at your wedding. You and your bridesmaids."

Susan clasped the bouquet of white and pink lilies to her breast. "They're beautiful. Thank you. I'm surprised you noticed what kind of flowers I carried at my wedding."

"I'm a very observant man. I've been trained to notice details." *Details like you're nervously adjusting your weight from foot to foot. Details like you answered the door immediately when I rang the bell, so that means you were eagerly waiting for me.*

"Please, come on back to the kitchen. I didn't see any reason for us to eat in the dining room." She motioned for him to follow her as she moved out of the foyer. "After all, it's not like this is a date. It's just a couple of friends having dinner together."

Who are you trying to convince, honey, you or me?

"Mmm-mmm, something sure smells good," he said as he entered the kitchen.

The room had been completely remodeled into a modern

kitchen. But the antique table, chairs and china cabinet added a touch of yesteryear. He watched as Susan tied a pink gingham apron around her waist and lifted the lid off a Crock-Pot. She looked right at home in the kitchen. A busy little housewife. Lowell must have loved being married to Susan. He'd been the kind of guy who'd always wanted a wife and kids and a simple, uncomplicated life in his hometown.

"Chicken stew," she said as she dipped the concoction into two huge bowls. "I made cornbread sticks to eat with it, but if you prefer crackers—"

"Cornbread sticks?" Hank licked his lips. "I remember your aunt Alice's cornbread sticks."

"I use her recipe. A pinch of this and a dab of that."

Susan placed the bowls on the floral place mats, poured their coffee and set the plate of cornbread sticks on the table. Then she arranged the lilies in a vase and set them in the center of the table. Hank pulled out her chair and seated her. She smiled at him and it was all he could do not to take her face in his hands and kiss her until she was breathless.

Did she have no idea how irresistible her sweet vulnerability was to him? How tempted he was to erase that almost virginal innocence from her eyes? And just how was it possible that a woman married for two years still projected an aura of inexperience?

"Do you remember Aunt Alice's Apple Dapple cake?" Susan asked.

"Do I? You've got to be kidding. Alice Williams's Apple Dapple cake was famous throughout Marshall County." He glanced across the table at Susan's intoxicating smile. "You don't mean you've baked me a cake."

"I thought you could take half of it up to the apartment with you and have it with coffee for breakfast in the morning."

"I'm not much of a breakfast eater, but I'll make an exception in this case."

The meal Susan had prepared was delicious and he ate until he was stuffed. He couldn't remember the last time he'd eaten so much. But then, he couldn't remember the last time a woman had prepared a home-cooked meal for him. Most of the ladies he dated had careers that left them little time for domestic chores. He'd never been attracted to the domestic type, had in fact steered clear of women who wanted to show him what good wife material they were.

His and Susan's conversation throughout the meal had been nothing more than idle chitchat. The weather. Aunt Alice's cooking. Susan's friendship with Tallie. How good the old house looked. Hank felt certain that Susan was trying as hard as he was to keep things light between them.

The minute Susan began clearing the table, Hank jumped up and took the dishes out of her hands. "Here, let me help."

"Just stack them in the sink," she said. "I'll put them in the dishwasher later. I imagine you'd like to see the apartment. Did you bring your things over tonight?"

He set the dishes down in the sink, wiped his hands off on a towel lying on the counter, then faced the woman who watched him with hungry eyes. *Don't look at me that way, honey,* he wanted to tell her. But he wasn't sure she realized how easily he could misinterpret her heated stare.

"Yeah, I'd like to see the place. And, yes, I brought my things. I didn't bring much with me from Alexandria."

"Come on, then, and I'll show you your new home."

When her two feisty dogs followed them to the back door, Susan turned and pointed her index finger at them. "No. Fred, you and Ricky aren't going with us. You two are staying here."

"Fred and Ricky?" Hank chuckled as he inspected the animals. "Good grief. I actually see a resemblance."

"Of course. Fred is round and fat and looks bald. I thought of Fred Mertz the first time I saw him. And of course, Ricky has those big black shoe-button eyes just like Ricky Ricardo."

"What about the cats? Don't tell me—"

"Lucy and Ethel."

Susan and Hank laughed together all the way out into the backyard and up the stairs to the garage apartment. She unlocked the door, walked inside and flipped the light switch.

Hank inspected the entire room in one glance. Neat. Clean. And small. His Alexandria apartment was three times the size. He'd probably feel a bit cramped at first, but he'd get used to the limited space. After all, living this close to Susan would be the easiest way to keep an eye on her.

"It's nice."

"I know it's small. The kitchenette is behind that screen over there. But it has a separate bedroom and nice little bathroom with a shower."

"How much room will I need anyway? This place seems to have all the essentials."

"The entrance is fairly private," she told him. "You can see the stairway and door from the back of my house, but the garage blocks a view of the entrance from the neighbors."

"Is there some reason you think I'd want the entrance to be that private?"

"Well, no, not really." Her cheeks flushed slightly. "It's just that if you decide you want to entertain someone—"

"A lady friend, you mean?"

"Yes, a lady friend. You're going to be living in

Crooked Oak for a whole year, so I assume you'll be dating on and off.''

''On and off,'' he repeated, then crossed his arms over his chest and looked directly at Susan. ''Would you mind— as my landlady, that is—if I brought female friends up here to the apartment?''

His question apparently took her off guard. She opened her mouth to speak, but only a long, sighing *oh* came out. She cleared her throat. ''It's none of my business if you choose to bring your dates back here.''

''To spend the night?'' He knew he should be ashamed of himself for taking such delight in flustering Susan this way. She seemed genuinely embarrassed discussing his love life.

''Hank, I—I...''

''I'll be very discreet.''

''Thank you. I'd appreciate that.''

''If you'd like, I can bring my date by your house and let you check her over. If you approve of her, she'll stay the night. If you give her a thumbs-down, then I'll take her home.''

Susan stared at him, seemingly speechless, for several minutes before she burst into laughter. ''Hank Bishop, I should skin you alive. You've been kidding me!'' Giggling like a schoolgirl, she headed straight for him. She swatted him on each arm in a playfully scolding manner. Laughing heartily, he slipped his arms around her. Then suddenly the laughter died and Hank became fully aware of how intimately he was holding her and how still she'd become.

He looked down into her eyes at the exact moment she lifted her face and stared up at him. All he could see was the yearning in those beautiful blue eyes and the temptation of those soft, pink lips.

She wanted him to kiss her, didn't she? If she didn't, why was she looking at him that way?

It would be the easiest thing in the world to pick her up in his arms and carry her to the bedroom. But a man didn't take a woman like Susan to bed unless he intended to make a commitment to her. A lifetime commitment.

He brushed a light kiss on her forehead, released his hold on her, then pushed her away. "Guess I'd better get my suitcase and garment bag. And I've got a couple of boxes with odds and ends in them."

"Do you need any help?"

"I don't want you lifting anything," he said. "You might not be showing yet, but you're still pregnant."

"Dr. Farr says that I'm as healthy as a horse."

"Who's Dr. Farr?"

"My obstetrician in Marshallton," she said. "The clinic in Nashville recommended that I choose a local OB-GYN to oversee my pregnancy."

"When do you see this Dr. Farr?"

"Today was the first time. I have another appointment in a month. And somewhere around five months, they'll do a sonogram and I can find out if the baby's a girl or boy then."

"So this Dr. Farr said you're okay. You and the baby."

"Perfectly fine."

"What do you want, a boy or a girl?" Hank asked.

"I don't really care. Lowell and I... We were just so happy that I was pregnant."

Silence hung heavily between them for several minutes, then Susan smiled at Hank and said, "Any time you'd like to go with me to one of my doctor's appointments, you're welcome to come. Maybe when I have the sonogram done, you'd like to be there."

Go with her to the OB-GYN's office when she had the sonogram done? Did he want to do that? Was that something a doting uncle or a godfather would do?

"Yeah, maybe. We'll see."

"Well, I'll let you get moved in. I've had a long day and I'm tired, so I'll see you tomorrow?"

"I'll walk you back—"

"No need. I do know the way."

He stood at the top of the stairs and watched her until she disappeared through the back door. What the hell had he gotten himself into? He had put his life on hold to come back home as a final payment on the debt he owed his best friend. He had known it wasn't going to be easy filling Lowell's shoes, even temporarily, but he had obligations and responsibilities he couldn't ignore. He was prepared to hunt down the man who had murdered Lowell and bring him to justice. He was prepared to keep an eye on Susan and make sure she and the baby were all right before he resumed his career. But he hadn't been prepared for the way Susan made him feel—for the way he wanted her.

One of the first things he needed to do, after he got settled in to the new job and the new apartment, was find himself a willing woman. The only way he was going to be able to keep his hands off Lowell's widow was by taking the edge off his desire—with someone else.

Four

He'd been living in the garage apartment two weeks now and had begun to settle into a routine at work. He stopped by every morning and every night to check on Susan, and they'd eaten a couple of meals together. Other than that, he kept his distance. Everyone in town expected him to step into Lowell's shoes, both personally and professionally. God knew he wanted to apprehend Lowell's murderer. And he was willing to complete his old friend's term as sheriff. But taking care of Lowell's wife was a complicated matter. If he didn't want her so damn bad... But he did. And that was the problem.

Tracking down Lowell's killer was the number one priority of the sheriff's department. Carl Bates seemed to have disappeared off the face of the earth, but Hank knew it was only a matter of time until one of their leads would uncover the white-trash drug pusher's whereabouts. Once they had the bastard in custody, the matter would be pretty much cut-and-dried. Two deputies had witnessed Lowell's murder. No jury on earth would render anything other than a guilty verdict. Yeah, once Bates was behind bars, his final fate would be the death penalty.

Where his professional duties were clear, Hank's personal obligations were not. His responsibility was to look after Susan. To protect her, not to bed her. But being around her on a daily basis, no matter how briefly, was playing hell with his libido.

As he gathered up his hunting gear and loaded it into the back of the old Jeep he'd bought at a local used car dealership, he thought seriously about leaving without checking on Susan this morning. After all, it was Sunday and awfully early. She might not even be up yet. One glance at the house and he knew she had to be awake. Lights were on in the kitchen. Maybe just a quick cup of coffee with her— although he hated the decaf stuff she was drinking these days—and he could meet Caleb for their hunting trip without feeling guilty that he hadn't made his daily morning call.

He knocked on the back door. No response. He knocked again. Nothing. Then he heard a sudden, loud yapping, the sound obviously coming from Fred and Ricky. Peering through the glass in the door, he surveyed the room. Empty, except for the two sniffing mutts eyeing the back door suspiciously. Maybe she'd gone back to bed and forgotten to turn off the light. If the dogs hadn't wakened her, then he wouldn't bother her. He'd stop back tonight, when he got home.

He turned and headed down the driveway, feeling as if he'd been given a reprieve. If he didn't see her this morning, maybe he wouldn't think about her during the day. Maybe thoughts of her wouldn't wreak havoc on his concentration. He didn't like this damn obsession he had with Lowell's widow. He had never allowed anyone or anything to influence the way he lived his life. Nobody snapped their fingers and told him to jump. Nobody!

Hell! Who was he kidding? Susan wasn't being demanding. The exact opposite was true. She seemed to sense his reluctance, his reserve, and hadn't asked him for anything.

He was the one with the problem. Not Susan.

"Hank?"

At the sound of her voice, he snapped his head around and looked at the open kitchen door. Wearing nothing but a gown, Susan stood just inside the doorway, her face pale, her hair disheveled. Ricky and Fred scurried past her and out onto the back porch. Guarding her. Issuing him a warning with their funny, ferocious little snarls.

"Morning. Sorry if I woke you." He didn't move. Barely breathed. He couldn't go inside and have a pleasant cup of coffee with a woman in her nightgown—not this woman.

"I've been awake for quite some time." Grasping the door frame, she closed her eyes. "I'm suffering a really severe bout of morning sickness. I was in the bathroom when you knocked."

Morning sickness? Yeah, sure, pregnant women upchucked fairly often in the first few months, didn't they? Although his knowledge of pregnancy was fairly limited, he thought he remembered something about eating crackers to ease the nausea.

"Have you tried crackers?" he asked.

"Crackers didn't help." She opened her eyes slowly and tried to smile.

"Why don't you call your doctor and have him prescribe something?"

"I may have to do that if it gets any worse."

"Anything I can do?" he asked, hoping she'd say no.

"No. Thanks." She glanced at the rifle and gear in the back of the Jeep. "Going hunting?"

"Yeah. Caleb and I thought it might be a good way to

spend some time together. I'll be back tonight. If it's not too late, I'll drop by.''

''You don't have to do that. I'll be perfectly—'' She gasped, covered her mouth with her hand and ran. Shadowing her every move, Ricky and Fred hightailed it after her.

Hell! She was sick again. She'll be okay, he told himself. She said so herself. Get a move on. She doesn't need you to hang around and play nursemaid.

Hank jumped into the Jeep, inserted the key and revved the motor. He sat there for a couple of minutes, the motor idling, while the morning sun shed its dawn cloak and exposed a new day to its naked brilliance.

What are you waiting for? Leave, dammit, man. Leave!

He killed the motor, shoved the keys into the pocket of his camouflage pants and jumped out of the Jeep. He stomped up the driveway and onto the back porch.

You're an idiot, Bishop.

After entering the kitchen, he closed the door behind him and went out into the hallway. ''Susan?''

She didn't reply, but she moaned.

He would rather face a pack of wolves than go into that bathroom. It wasn't as if he could actually do anything for her. If the situation was reversed, the last thing he'd want would be for her to try to soothe him. But she was a woman, dammit, and women were different. They wanted and expected to be soothed and pampered when they were sick. Especially pregnant women. Right?

When he saw her on her knees in front of the commode, he stopped abruptly in the doorway. Damn, she looked vulnerable. Small. Helpless. And pitifully sick.

''Susan?''

Ricky and Fred sniffed at his legs. He gently eased past them.

Susan glanced up at him with teary eyes. A tight knot

formed in the pit of his belly. She opened her mouth to speak, but turned suddenly and threw up again.

"Honey, what can I do?" he asked.

She rolled tissue from the holder and used it to wipe her mouth, then tossed it into the bowl and flushed the commode. "Could you get me a wet washcloth?"

"Sure thing." Reluctantly he stepped farther inside the spacious bathroom and looked around, searching for the linen closet. Finding it to his right, he opened the door, reached inside to the neatly arranged shelves and retrieved a cloth. While he dampened the cloth, he glanced over at her. Sweat coated her pale face and moistened her cotton gown. There was a soft, pleading look in her eyes.

He knelt beside her, handed her the washcloth and resisted the urge to wipe her face himself.

"Thank you." She washed her face, tossed the cloth into the sink and then wrapped her arms around her stomach.

"Still sick?"

She nodded. "I'm cramping."

"Is that normal? I mean, is cramping a part of morning sickness?"

"No, not that I know of." She held out her hand to him. "Help me stand up, please. I'd better get in touch with Dr. Farr."

"Do you think something's wrong, more than morning sickness, I mean?"

"I'm cramping and spotting a little and… Oh, Hank, I'm really worried."

He lifted her into his arms. She gasped. "It's all right, honey. You're going to bed and I'm calling Dr. Farr myself."

"His number is by the phone on my nightstand," she said. "You'll get his service when you call, so you'll have to leave a message."

Hank laid her on the unmade bed, sat on the edge and

picked up the telephone. He opened the pad on the night-stand and found the obstetrician's number. While the phone rang, he glanced back over his shoulder at Susan.

"You've got cramps, you're spotting, and you've been vomiting. Anything else?"

"No, that about covers it."

The minute the service responded, Hank explained the situation and asked for the doctor to return his call immediately.

Susan lifted her hand and placed it on Hank's arm. He jumped. "Thank you. I'll be okay, if you want to go on and meet Caleb. I'm sure Dr. Farr will call back very soon."

"Oh, hell, I forgot all about Caleb. I need to call him to let him know… Do you have call waiting?"

"Yes."

He pulled Susan's hand off his arm and clasped it tightly in his. He gave it a reassuring squeeze. "I'm not going anywhere until I know you're okay." Hank dialed his brother's number.

"Hello?" Caleb answered.

"It's me," Hank said. "I can't make it this morning. Susan's sick. We're waiting for the doctor to return our call."

"What's wrong?"

"Cramping. Spotting. And severe vomiting."

"Do you want Sheila and me to come over?" Caleb asked.

"No, thanks. I think we can handle things. I'll talk to you later."

"Sure thing."

Susan slid over to the edge of the bed and tried to stand. Hank replaced the telephone receiver quickly, then grabbed her by the arm.

"I'm sick again," she told him.

"Hold on, honey."

He swept her up into his arms and ran toward the bathroom. The minute he put her on her feet, she leaned over the commode and emptied her stomach.

"Oh, Lord, Hank!" She gasped for air. "I'm so sick."

Supporting her around the waist with one arm, he reached over and turned on the sink faucets so he could dampen the washcloth. He wiped her mouth and chin, then dumped the cloth into the sink.

"I'm not waiting for the doctor to call back," he told her. "I'm taking you to the emergency room right now."

She nodded, but only slightly, as if the movement caused her pain. "I think that's a good idea." She grabbed the front of his shirt. "I'm scared. I'm afraid something's wrong with the baby. What—" she swallowed her tears "—what if I'm miscarrying?"

"We're going to the hospital. I'll call Dr. Farr's service again and tell them to have him meet us. Everything's going to be okay." He walked her over to the vanity stool, sat her down and clasped her chin. "Stay right here, in case you get sick again. I'll be right back with your coat and shoes. Don't move. I'll carry you to the car."

All the way to the hospital, he kept thinking about the possibility that Susan might miscarry. Maybe it would be better if she did. Lowell had wanted to be a father. He didn't. But Lowell wasn't around anymore to see his wife through her pregnancy and to be a dad to the child she was carrying. If Susan lost the baby, then he wouldn't have to be responsible for her or the child. Once he finished Lowell's term as sheriff, he could leave Crooked Oak and Susan behind him. Without the child, there was nothing to bind him to her.

The endless minutes of waiting in the emergency room seemed like hours. What the hell was taking them so long?

"Sheriff Bishop, you can come back in now," the gray-haired nurse informed him. "Dr. Farr has finished examining Mrs. Redman and she's asking for you."

He hesitated momentarily. What if she'd lost the baby? What if he was going to have to comfort her and try to convince her that it had been for the best?

Hank opened the door to the examining room, took a deep breath and looked inside to find Susan sitting on the edge of a padded table. She glanced up at him and smiled. That could only mean one thing. He felt as if he'd been punched in the belly with an iron fist.

Thank God, she hasn't lost the baby! Where had that thought come from? he wondered. Surely not from the same logical mind that had, only moments before, rationalized the benefits of a miscarriage. On some elemental, totally primitive level, he must want the child.

"The baby's fine," Susan said.

"What about you?" Hank asked.

"Susan's going to be all right," Dr. Farr said. "She's picked up a stomach virus somewhere and that is what's causing the cramping and severe vomiting."

"What about the spotting?" Hank looked directly at the doctor.

"It's perfectly normal for a woman to spot a little during the first trimester. It's nothing to worry about. We've given her an injection that should help ease the symptoms of the virus. She needs to drink clear fluids and get some rest." Dr. Farr turned to Susan. "Now, little mother, you can stop worrying. I want you to go home, rest and relax. If you aren't feeling a lot better by this afternoon, call me and I'll make a house call."

"To make a promise like that, you must be certain that I'm going to be okay." Susan laughed.

Dr. Farr patted Hank on the shoulder as he paused beside

him on his way out of the examining room. "I'm glad you're around to look after Susan. She's going to need a good man to take care of her for the next seven months."

Forcing a smile, Hank nodded.

"Is it too late for you and Caleb to go hunting?" Susan asked. "I feel terrible that I kept you from enjoying a day out in the cold, damp woods with your brother."

Hank narrowed his gaze. "I'd forgotten that you aren't an advocate of hunting."

"I'm not a rabble-rouser," Susan said. "Anyone who wants to kill poor, defenseless animals has every right to do so. I just can't understand the reasoning that enables people to get pleasure out of it."

Hank lifted her coat off the rack and draped it around her shoulders. "Come on, little mother. Let's go home."

Hank opened two cans of cat food and dumped them into the small ceramic bowls decorated with roses and inscribed with the names Lucy and Ethel. Susan's felines watched and waited, neither coming near their bowls until Hank moved away to lift the sack of dog food from the pantry shelf. Fred and Ricky lay on the large braided rug by the table, intently staring at the stainless steel dishes engraved with their names.

When he'd put Susan to bed earlier that day, she'd asked him to feed her animals around six o'clock, if she wasn't able to get up and do it herself. It was after six and Susan was still sleeping. She'd slept nearly all day, thanks to the shot the doctor had given her.

Hank washed his hands, then poured himself a cup of freshly brewed coffee—regular that he'd retrieved from his apartment. Returning to the den, he relaxed in the large, brown leather recliner and turned the sound up on the television enough to hear the local news and weather report.

He had spent the afternoon watching a football game on

TV and periodically checking on Susan. Twice, he'd found her without any cover. Apparently she still had a little fever and was kicking back the sheet and quilt when she got hot. Each time he'd been unable to keep from inspecting her. Slender curves. Small, delicate bone structure. Small round breasts that seemed to enlarge more and more each week. Just looking at her, no one would suspect she was pregnant.

As Hank leaned back in the recliner, his stomach growled. He'd fixed himself a sandwich for lunch, but that had been hours ago. What he'd like was a thick steak and a big baked potato. He could call Steak Express in Marshallton, but he wasn't sure they delivered all the way to Crooked Oak.

"Hank?"

He jumped at the sound of her voice. His heartbeat accelerated. He got up and hurried down the hall. After easing open the door a fraction, he poked his head into her bedroom. She was sitting up in bed, the pillows propped behind her back. Color had returned to her face and she was smiling.

"Feeling better?" he asked.

"Much better, thank you."

"You're looking a lot better." He pushed the door open all the way, but didn't enter the room. Instead, he leaned his hip against the doorjamb and crossed his arms over his chest. "So, what do you need?"

"Have you been here all day?"

"Yep."

"You didn't have to stay."

"I wanted to stay," he admitted, as much to himself as to her. "Just in case you needed me. After all, that's one of the reasons I'm in Crooked Oak, isn't it—to look after you?"

"What have you been doing to pass the time?"

"Watching football." Why the hell did she have to look

so damn good? Most women, after a severe bout with a stomach virus, would look terrible. But not Susan. With her long, brown hair a ratty mess and her face void of any makeup, she looked sweet and sexy. That was it—that was why he found her so attractive. That contradictory combination of sweet, innocent wholesomeness and hot, tempting sexuality. She probably had no idea how sexy she was. Or how much he wanted her.

"Oh, yeah, I fed the zoo," he said. "They're out in the kitchen lapping it up right now."

"The zoo?" Susan giggled. "You call two cats and two dogs a zoo? If you really want to see a zoo, stop by the shelter sometime."

"Working around all those animals isn't a problem, is it?" he asked. "I mean, being exposed to them and you pregnant. I've heard they can carry diseases, especially cats."

"That's true. Cats can carry something called toxoplasmosis, which is dangerous to the fetus. But Scooter oversees most of the hands-on work at the shelter, now that I'm pregnant. And I always wear disposable gloves here at home when I change the litter boxes, and at work when I come in contact with the animals."

"Sorry, I didn't mean for my questions to sound like I'm trying to interfere with—"

"I appreciate your concern," she said. "It's sweet of you to care."

"Of course, I care. You're Lowell's wife and one of Tallie's best friends." That's it, Bishop, he told himself. Let her know that you don't have any personal feelings for her.

"Yes, I'm Lowell's widow," she said quietly. "I'm sorry, Hank, that my pregnancy has complicated your life. That Lowell's death brought you home to temporarily take over his responsibilities."

Hank uncrossed his arms. "That's not your fault. None of us knew, when I agreed to...to do Lowell a favor, that he was going to get killed a month later." Damn, but this conversation was making him uncomfortable. "Even if you hadn't been pregnant, I probably would have agreed to come back and finish out Lowell's term as sheriff. I want to see his killer caught and punished."

"But my being pregnant and the child being..." She lowered her gaze as she stroked the patchwork quilt that covered her from the waist down. "Your being my baby's biological father no doubt makes you feel more responsible than you would have if Lowell had been the father."

What could he say? How did he respond to her statement? Of course, knowing the child she carried was his doubled—no, tripled—his feelings of responsibility.

"Do you regret agreeing to the artificial insemination?" she asked. "I mean, now that Lowell—"

"I never wanted to be a father that's for sure." Damn, he hadn't meant to speak so sharply. He walked into the room and toward the bed, but he stopped several feet away from her. "Look, Susan, I have no intentions of marrying and producing any kids of my own. When I agreed to donate my sperm so that you and Lowell could have a baby, I never for one minute thought I'd wind up having to step in and try to be a father to the child. I'm not sure I can. I'll do my best to look after you for the next seven months and I'll always be available if you need me. But I can't be more than a godfather to your baby."

"I understand," she said.

"I'll take an interest, of course. Birthday presents and Christmas presents. And when he's older, he can come visit me. And—"

"I said I understand," she repeated, her voice an octave higher.

"Okay. Fine. I'm glad you do." He shoved his hands

into his pockets and rocked back and forth on his heels. "So, is there anything you want or need right now?"

"I'm hungry."

"Hungry?"

"Do you suppose you could fix me some creamed potatoes? Whenever I was sick as a child, Aunt Alice would always fix me creamed potatoes."

"Creamed potatoes, huh? I'm not much of a cook, but if that's what you want, I'll give it a try."

"Thank you."

He wished she wouldn't look at him so appreciatively with those big blue eyes of hers. He didn't want to feed her—he wanted to make love to her.

"It'll take me a while," he said. "Anything else you need before I tackle the potatoes."

"No, thanks. I think I can make it to the bathroom by myself."

She threw back the covers, slid her legs to the side of the bed and, using her hands braced on the bed's edge as leverage, lifted herself to her feet. Her gown, which had been hiked up to midthigh, dropped to her ankles, covering the smooth satin of her naked flesh. Hank's sex grew hard and heavy. He turned quickly and left the room.

"I'll be back with your potatoes as soon as I can," he shouted from the hallway.

Susan shook her head as sadness and humor combined within her. Hank Bishop was afraid of her! The realization surprised her. He was as scared of her as she had always been of him. But why? What sort of threat could she possibly be to him?

He doesn't want to be a father, an inner voice reminded her. *And you* are *carrying his baby.*

"He doesn't want to love this child." She patted her

tummy as she walked to the bathroom. "He's afraid of caring about me and our baby."

Just as Susan finished using the bathroom, she heard Hank's Jeep. Where was he going? He hadn't said a word about leaving. Maybe he was going out to try to find some creamed potatoes. Surely not. The nearest restaurant open on a Sunday night was over in Marshallton.

She glanced at herself in the mirror and cringed. I need a bath! But she felt as weak as a wet dishrag. What if she fell in the shower?

After a quick sponge bath at the sink, Susan brushed her teeth, combed her hair and changed her gown. By the time she sat down in the wingback chair beside the window in her bedroom, she heard the Jeep pull into the driveway. Fred and Ricky barked a couple of times, and Hank scolded them. Susan smiled. His voice sounded rough and mean, but she knew, from personal experience, that like Ricky and Fred, Hank's bark was worse than his bite.

She sat in the big chair, trying to relax, trying not to think about anything beyond today. Hank might not want his baby and he might not want her. Not now. Not yet. But right this minute, he was in her kitchen, fixing her something to eat. He was soothing her. Petting her. Taking care of her. She doubted that he'd ever tried to pacify another woman the way he was trying so hard to pacify her.

Susan smiled. A contented smile. Rome wasn't built in a day, she reminded herself. Conquering her own fears and Hank's might take some time, but for the sake of the baby growing inside her, she had to find a way. In seven months, she and Hank were going to become parents—whether or not either of them was ready for the awesome responsibility.

He rapped softly on the bedroom door.

"Yes?"

"Your creamed potatoes are ready," he said.

"Great. I'm starved. Come on in."

She glanced up when he approached the chair and for one split second was taken back by the sight of Hank Bishop carrying a shiny stainless steel stew pot in his hand. A long wooden spoon stuck straight up in the middle of the pot. Hank handed her a dish towel and then offered her the pot. She couldn't suppress a grin.

"They're instant potatoes," he admitted. "I ran down to the grocery store and picked up a box. I followed the instructions, but they look a bit lumpy to me."

"I'm sure they're delicious," she told him, accepting the offering and managing not to giggle.

She lifted the spoon. The concoction stuck to the utensil's surface. She eyed the potatoes.

"Is there something wrong with them?" he asked.

"Oh, no. They're fine." Susan put the spoon to her mouth and licked off a bite of the thick, white glob. Despite the uneven texture of the potatoes, they didn't taste half bad. Of course, she *was* starving to death.

Hank stood and watched her as she ate several bites, then he relaxed. She noted the way his tense shoulders eased and the frown on his face was replaced by a self-satisfied smile.

Men! Susan thought. Especially hard-edged, macho types like Hank. He would never admit that her approval was important to him. That he wanted very much to please her. Perhaps he wasn't even aware of it himself.

She ate about a fifth of the instant potatoes, then handed the pot to Hank. "They were delicious, but that's all my stomach will hold right now. Thank you, Hank, for being so good to me."

Was that a blush she saw coloring his cheeks? Susan wondered. It was! She'd embarrassed him. She smiled, barely suppressing the laughter bubbling up inside her.

When he took the pot from her, she deliberately allowed

their hands to touch. Sizzling, shivering contact. He looked into her eyes and for one brief moment she thought he was going to kiss her. He grabbed the pot out of her hand and stepped backward, moving quickly away from her.

"I'll clean up in the kitchen and then I'll head on—"

"Hank?"

"Yeah?" He halted in his hasty retreat.

"I know it would be an imposition, but…well, would it be asking too much for you to stay here tonight? I have four bedrooms upstairs. You could take your pick."

"Do you really need me to stay? I'll be right next door. You could call if—"

"Forget I asked. I guess I'm just feeling nervous after the scare about the baby."

"I can stick around for a while, if it would make you feel better. Until bedtime."

"All right. Thank you. And I really am sorry about asking you to stay here. I'd promised myself that I wouldn't be a burden to you. That I wouldn't take up too much of your time or interfere in your life. And here I am, only two months pregnant, and already making unreasonable demands."

"Asking me to stay overnight wasn't an unreasonable demand," he said, his back to her. "If it'll make you feel better, I'll stay."

"You don't have to do that. Really you don't."

"I'm staying." He left the room.

End of discussion. Final decision. That's it. Susan smiled as she wrapped her arms around her waist.

"Your daddy's going to spend the night with us, little one."

Five

The best way to get one woman off your mind is with another woman, Hank had told himself. He was allowing Susan to get too close to him. Thoughts of her occupied too much of his time and that was a dangerous thing. He could hardly make advances to his best friend's widow—especially not this soon. Lowell had been dead only two months. But if he didn't put some space between himself and Susan, he wasn't sure what might happen.

And that was why he'd let his deputy, Richard Holman, fix him up on a blind date.

Hank chuckled. God, he must be desperate! He'd never gone on a blind date, not even in high school. But a man did what a man had to do.

Lucky for him, Kendra Camp turned out to be a damn good-looking woman. Tall and leggy. Not too old, but not too young. About thirty, he guessed. A divorcée with no kids.

He'd taken her to Marshallton for dinner and dancing. And she'd been the one to suggest they go back to his place. It wasn't that he was opposed to sex on a first date; he'd even had a couple of one-night stands in the past. But this wasn't Washington, D.C., or Alexandria. This was Crooked Oak, Tennessee, and he was the sheriff. If Kendra stayed overnight, tongues would wag. So, she wouldn't stay overnight, he told himself as he escorted her up the stairs to his front door. He reached around her and undid the lock. She turned, smiled at him and kissed him. He pulled her into his arms and deepened the kiss.

She pulled back from him. "Maybe we'd better go inside."

"Yeah, maybe we should."

He flipped on the light, shoved his keys into his pocket and then helped Kendra out of her coat. While he removed his coat and laid his and hers on a nearby chair, she kicked off her heels and curled up on his sofa.

"You want something to drink?" he asked. "Beer or whiskey?"

"Beer would be fine." She glanced around his apartment. "Don't you feel kind of cramped in this little place?"

He opened the refrigerator, retrieved two beers and opened the caps. "Want a glass for your beer?" She shook her head and mouthed the word no. "It's about half the size of my place in Alexandria, but it's convenient living next door to Susan. I can check on her every day and I'm close in case she needs me."

"Susan is Lowell Redman's widow, isn't she? I hear she's pregnant. Must be really rough on her losing her husband like that." Kendra accepted the beer Hank offered her.

He sat beside her, lifted the bottle to his mouth and downed a hefty swig. Why the hell had he mentioned Susan? The purpose of this date with Kendra was to get his mind off the tempting Mrs. Redman.

"She has a lot of friends," Hank said. "A lot of people who care about her. She and the baby will be all right."

"She's certainly lucky to have you." Kendra placed her beer on the coffee table, slid closer to Hank, draped her arm around his shoulders and smiled seductively. "And from what I hear, so is Marshall County. Not many men would take a leave of absence from a big important FBI job to come back to live in a hick town, just to look after their best friend's widow."

"Lowell and I were best friends since we were kids. He even saved my life once, when we were teenagers. There wasn't anything I wouldn't have done for him."

Kendra snuggled closer, pressing her body against his, tilting her head so that her lips almost touched his. "Well, I for one am glad you're back in Tennessee. I think I'm going to enjoy having you around."

Hank put his beer bottle down beside hers. More than ready to accept what she was offering, he pulled her into his arms. As he claimed her lips, he eased her backward, down into the plush sofa cushions. Then he heard a light rapping at the door and a soft feminine voice calling his name, but before he could untangle himself from Kendra or wipe her mauve lipstick off his face, Susan opened the door and walked into the room.

"I noticed your car was back so I thought I'd come over and see if you wanted—" Susan stopped dead-still after she'd taken only a few steps. Her cheeks flushed scarlet. She began backing toward the door. "Oh, I'm so sorry. I didn't know you... I had no idea. Please forgive me for intruding."

Susan turned and fled. Hank practically tossed Kendra onto the floor when he jumped up and ran after Susan. Kendra let out a loud yelp as she grabbed the sofa arm to steady herself. By the time Hank made it halfway down the stairs, Susan was long gone. The sound of her back door slamming reverberated in his ears.

Damn! He stood there for a few minutes, trying to figure out the wisest course of action. He had two women on his hands—both of whom were probably mad as hell at him, and he didn't blame either of them. He should have told Susan he had a date tonight. And he should have locked the damn front door! He'd have to apologize to Kendra for leaving her so abruptly. He'd acted on pure instinct when he'd run after Susan.

When Hank walked back upstairs to his apartment, he found Kendra slipping into her coat. Hell, he'd blown it big time! Putting on his best apologetic face, he looked at her and felt a modicum of relief when she smiled at him.

"I'm sorry." He took a couple of tentative steps in her direction. "You don't have to leave."

"Oh, yes, I do." Reaching out, Kendra caressed his cheek. "I like you, Hank. But I make it a policy not to date guys who are already involved with someone else."

"Whoa, there," he said. "Wait just a minute. I'm not involved with—"

Kendra placed her index finger over his lips, silencing him. "Oh, yes, you are. Maybe you don't even realize it. But from where I'm standing, I can see it plainly. Susan Redman was more than embarrassed to find us making out on your couch. She was angry and jealous. Believe me, a woman senses these things in another woman."

"You're wrong. Susan doesn't—"

Kendra laughed. "Yes, she does. And so do you. You wouldn't have tossed me aside and run after her, if you didn't."

"I was worried about her being upset," Hank explained lamely. "She's pregnant and—"

Kendra gave him a quick kiss. "Come on. Take me

home. By the time you get back, she'll have cooled off and
you can go talk to her.''

"I don't owe Susan an explanation for my actions."
Hank put on his coat. "My life is my own." He followed
Kendra outside, locked the door and walked down the stairs
behind her. "I'm free to do whatever I want, with whom-
ever I want." He assisted Kendra into the Lexus, rounded
the hood and got in on the driver's side. "She had no business barging in the way she did."

"Yeah. Sure," was all Kendra said when he started the
engine and backed the Lexus out of the driveway.

Thirty minutes later, after depositing Kendra safely at her
front door, he came home, parked his car and sat behind
the wheel as he stared at the back of Susan's house.

Why should he care what she thought? It was none of
her business if he chose to fool around with half the women
in Marshall County. And she was the one who had barged
in on him—uninvited and unannounced!

She had run away because she'd been embarrassed and
that was all there was to it. Kendra was dead wrong if she
thought Susan had been angry and jealous. The very idea
was ridiculous.

Or was it?

If he wanted Susan, then why was it out of the question
that she wanted him, too? Because she's Lowell's wife,
dammit! His widow, he corrected himself immediately. But
she still loves Lowell. I'm sure of it.

So what if she still loves Lowell? his inner voice argued.
*That doesn't mean she doesn't have needs, that she doesn't
want you every bit as much as you want her.*

Don't go there, Bishop, he warned himself. This is Susan
Williams Redman we're talking about here. This is no temporary kind of woman. You take her to bed and she's going
to expect a commitment. And Hank Bishop doesn't make
commitments.

He got out of the Lexus and headed toward the garage apartment, then stopped suddenly when he heard Susan's back door open and footsteps on the porch. Don't turn around, he told himself. Just keep walking. Pretend you didn't hear anything.

"Hank."

Damn! "Yeah?" He kept his back to her.

"I'm sorry about what happened. I had no idea you had a date."

"I should have mentioned it to you," he said.

"I hope you explained to your date who I was and what our relationship is. I wouldn't want her getting the wrong idea about why I came barging into your apartment that way."

He turned slowly and faced her. She had left the porch light off, and only the light coming through the open kitchen door illuminated her body. She stood there on the edge of the porch, wrapped snugly in an ankle-length terry-cloth robe, her hair hanging freely across her shoulders. His body tensed at the sight of her. How the hell had he gotten himself into this situation? he asked himself for the hundredth time. He wasn't going to be able to walk away and leave her, which would have been the sensible thing to do.

"Sorry I didn't get a chance to introduce you two," he said. "Her name's Kendra Camp. She's a nurse at County General. She works with Richard Holman's wife and they set up the date for us."

"That was nice of them." Hugging herself, Susan rubbed her hands up and down her arms.

"Yeah, it was." He took a hesitant step toward her. "Are you cold? Maybe you should go back inside before you—"

"Why didn't you tell me this morning that you had a date tonight?"

"Guess it just slipped my mind." *Liar! You deliberately didn't tell her.* But why? Hell, he didn't know why! He wasn't used to having to dissect the reason for his actions or to justify them to anyone.

"If I'd known, I wouldn't have...I'd never have barged in on you the way I did." Her body shivered ever so slightly.

He closed the distance between them, wrapped his arm around her shoulders and turned her toward the back door. "Come on, let's go inside, honey. You're freezing to death out here."

She felt like such a total fool! She had intruded on his privacy as if she had a right to do it. And she had interrupted him and his date, who were going at it hot and heavy on the sofa. Just the memory of Hank kissing and fondling the woman renewed the blazing anger and raging jealousy she had experienced.

She had no claims on Hank. He wasn't her husband or her lover. She had no right to be angry or jealous when she caught him practically making love to another woman.

Susan allowed Hank to lead her inside and seat her at the kitchen table. He swept back a strand of errant hair that had fallen across her left eye. She sucked in her breath. He withdrew his hand. She looked up at him, but before she could read the expression in his dark eyes, he turned from her.

"How about some hot chocolate?" he asked.

"I'll fix us some," she said.

"You stay put, little mother. I know where everything is."

She wished Hank hadn't picked up on Dr. Farr's generic nickname for all his pregnant patients. *Little mother.* On Hank's lips the words sounded like an endearment. She preferred the casual *honey* instead.

While Hank busied himself preparing the hot chocolate,

Susan removed her heavy terry-cloth robe and draped it over the chair. The gown underneath was a sensible, long-sleeved flannel. Sensible and warm. Certainly not sexy or alluring.

She didn't want to be sexy and alluring for Hank anyway. *Liar*, her conscience mocked her. *No matter how much the thought of gaining Hank Bishop's full attention still scares the hell out of you, you can't deny the fact that you want him—now more than ever.*

And he was still just as dangerous to her as he ever was. The way she felt about him—the way she always felt about him—was the same way she imagined her mother had felt about her father. Wild, uncontrollable passion. Aunt Alice had warned her about where those kinds of feelings would lead her. Down the same path her mother had taken—straight to an unwed pregnancy and desertion.

"If she had waited for a proper young man, someone safe and sensible, she could have saved herself a great deal of heartache and you from growing up without a father," Aunt Alice had said. "Passions that intense always come to no good. You remember that, child. That kind of love burns itself out and then you have nothing left."

At the time, Susan hadn't realized that Aunt Alice had been talking about herself as well as Susan's mother. Years later, when she was sick and dying, she'd confessed to Susan that she'd been in love once, long ago, with a very unsuitable young man.

"When he touched me, I trembled," Alice had said. "I adored him. Worshiped him. Thought of him night and day. And he told me that he felt the same way about me. But his passion burned out very quickly, after we became lovers. He left me. Moved on to other women."

Did she have the courage to risk losing her heart and her pride to find out what it would be like to belong to Hank? Could she now, as a grown woman, ignore her aunt's warnings and accept the way she felt, pursue what she had always wanted and allow passion to overrule her common sense?

"Here you go. One hot chocolate," Hank said, placing the mug of cocoa in front of her on the table.

"What?" His voice brought her abruptly out of the foggy haze of her thoughts. "Oh, yes. Thank you, Hank." Forcing a smile to her lips, she lifted the warm mug in her hands.

With an identical red mug in one hand, he pulled out a chair from the table with the other. Crossing his legs, ankle over knee, he leaned back and brought the cocoa to his mouth. He drank a few sips of the rich, sweet liquid, all the while eyeing her over the rim of the mug.

"Drink up," he said.

She sipped the cocoa. Warmth spread down her throat and into her belly. "Hank, I want to apologize again, about disrupting your date. I hope Ms. Camp didn't leave early on my account. You did explain to her about our relationship, didn't you?"

Hank set the mug on the table a little harder than he'd intended. The dark, creamy liquid sloshed over the sides and onto the floral place mat. "And just what is our relationship? What should I have told my date? 'Oh, don't pay any attention to the way Susan ran out of my apartment in a huff after she caught us making out. Lowell's widow and I are just friends. You must have misunderstood her reaction. She wasn't jealous. She has no reason to be. You see, even though Susan is pregnant with *my* baby, she and I have never had a sexual relationship!'"

All she could do was sit there, mouth agape, startled eyes open wide, and stare across the table at him. Dear Lord, he knew. He knew she'd been jealous when she'd seen another woman in his arms. And his date—this Kendra Camp—had known, too.

"Is that what you thought...what she thought? That I was jealous." Susan forced a shrill, fake laugh. "I was embarrassed, that's—"

Hank shot up from the chair and rounded the table so quickly that Susan's breath caught in her throat. He towered over her, his face tense, his jaw taut. For one tiny instant, she was afraid of him. Afraid of the rage she saw in his black eyes.

"Don't you dare lie to me." He spoke through clenched teeth.

He was angry with her. But why? Because she'd been jealous? Because her reaction had driven away his date? Or because she was trying so hard to hide the way she truly felt?

"What do you want me to say?" she asked, her heart beating wildly.

"I want you to tell me the truth," he said. "Don't you think it's time we both faced the truth and quit trying to pretend there's nothing going on between us."

"But there isn't anything going on between us." She shook her head in denial.

"You're pregnant with my child. I think that constitutes—"

"A child that was never meant to be yours." Susan gripped the edge of the table with white-knuckled strength. "You don't want this child. You think you owe it to Lowell to look after me now and be around for my child after it's born. You're just here because you're trying to act responsibly."

Hank reached down, placed his hands at her waist and lifted her to her feet. She struggled momentarily, then ceased her movements and stood perfectly still. "All that you said is true enough," he told her as he cupped her face between his two big hands, forcing her to look directly at him. "But I'm not talking about the baby or Lowell or responsibility. I'm talking about what's been going on between us ever since I came back to Crooked Oak for Lowell's funeral.''

"Nothing's been going on—''

He ran his thumb over her lips. "I've pretended it wasn't there. I've tried to deny it. But trying to ignore it isn't going to make it go away.''

"Please.'' Tears gathered in her eyes. "Please, don't do this.''

He kissed her forehead. "Do you think I want to feel this way?'' He kissed one of her cheeks and then the other. Sweet, tender kisses. She trembled from head to toe. "Do you think it's easy for me to admit that I want my best friend's widow? That every time I'm around you, I get hard just thinking about making love to you?''

Susan opened her mouth to speak, but all that came out was a choked gasp. Tears spilled from her eyes, ran down her face and onto his hands.

"You want me, too, don't you, honey?'' When she tried to lower her head, he urged her face upward until she met his gaze. "You're as hungry for me as I am for you.''

"I can't…I can't…'' Didn't he understand what it would mean if she admitted how she felt about him? Didn't he know that the only thing standing between the two of them—the only thing keeping them from becoming lovers—was her fear? If she ever succumbed to her emotions, ever gave herself to him completely, she'd be lost.

Loving Lowell had been safe and simple and easy. She'd never had to give him everything—her whole heart, her total passion, her very soul. Lowell had accepted and been content with what she'd been able to give him. But Hank would never be satisfied with half a portion. He'd want it all. And he'd take it. And when he left her—as he was sure to do one day—she'd have nothing.

She had to convince him that he was wrong, that he'd

misunderstood her actions these past two months. She opened her mouth to speak, to once again deny her innermost feelings, but before she could utter a word, his lips covered hers in a kiss that allowed no refusal. Hot and hard and demanding. He grasped the back of her neck with one big hand and used the other hand to cup her hip and press her intimately against his arousal. She tried to resist, tried valiantly to refuse him, but her body betrayed her. Her weak, sex-starved body surrendered completely.

She had spent a lifetime dreaming about being in Hank Bishop's arms. He had been her first love—secret though it was. She had yearned for him as only a teenage girl can yearn. She had envied every woman he'd ever touched, ever kissed.

She had loved him from afar—from a safe distance—but all the while she'd wondered what his lips tasted like, what he smelled like, how his body would feel against hers. And now she knew. And the reality far exceeded her expectations.

The kiss deepened and intensified, going on and on, until she thought she'd die from the pleasure. She reached out for him. Clung to him. Pressed her tender breasts against his hard chest. Allowed him to bring her up and brush her mound against his throbbing sex.

She barely recognized the husky, breathy sound she heard as a sexual moan escaping from her own lips. When he covered one breast with the palm of his hand and gently kneaded, she groaned with pleasure and then came apart in his arms when he rotated his thumb over her nipple. Even through the layer of her flannel gown, the sensation inflamed her.

She was fast losing control and so was he. If she didn't stop him now, there would be no turning back. Hank was going to make love to her. A war raged inside her. Desire battling with common sense.

He doesn't love you, she reminded herself, while she still could manage a rational thought. He only wants you. You cannot take him into your body, allow him to become your lover and escape unharmed.

When he moved his lips down her neck, edging closer and closer to the vee of flesh revealed by the top two undone buttons of her gown, Susan realized she had to do something to stop him. It was the most difficult thing she'd ever done.

Shoving against his chest, she said, "No, please. I can't. We can't." Using the most logical explanation for why they couldn't act on their feelings, she told him, "Lowell…Lowell's only been dead two months."

She had known before she spoke that the mention of Lowell would bring their interlude to a halt. Quickly. Painfully.

Hank glared at her, his eyes hazed by passion. Breathing hard, his chest rising and falling rapidly, he withdrew from her—first emotionally, then mentally, and finally physically.

Without saying a word, he turned, walked across the kitchen and out the back door. Susan slumped into a chair before her knees gave way. She laid her head atop her crossed arms on the table. When the reality of how close she'd come to fulfilling a lifelong dream—of possessing and being possessed by Hank Bishop—hit her, she sobbed. She wasn't sure how long she sat there, crying her heart out, but eventually she became aware of Ethel and Lucy curling about her legs. She reached down to stroke them and noticed Fred and Ricky sitting at her feet, staring up at her. Despite the presence of her precious pets, she had never felt so alone.

She caressed her tummy. But she wasn't alone. Hank might never belong to her, might never love her, but a part of him—his child—would belong to her forever.

* * *

The next morning she was sitting at the kitchen table, eating a bowl of cereal, when Hank knocked on the back door. She hadn't expected him to make his routine morning visit. Not after what had happened between them last night.

"Come in," she said. "The door's unlocked."

Hank opened the door, but hovered just inside the doorway. "Are you all right?"

She nodded. "Yes, I'm all right."

"I just stopped by to tell you that I'm going to start looking for another apartment," he said, his gaze riveted to the floor.

"Oh, I see."

"I thought, after what happened last night, it would be better if I wasn't living so close by." He lifted his gaze and looked directly at her. "Don't you agree?"

"I—I don't know." She was going to lose him completely now. Because she'd been afraid to give herself to him. Because she'd used her husband—his best friend—as an excuse to not succumb to his lovemaking. She couldn't bear the thought that he was leaving her.

Better now than later, she told herself. It'll hurt now, but later, if we became lovers, it would destroy me when he left.

"Are you saying you want me to stay?" he asked.

"Yes...no..." She turned her face so that she didn't have to look into his eyes. "You're right. You should look for somewhere else to live. Offering you the garage apartment was a bad idea. I should have known..."

"I'll start looking for another apartment right away," he said. "I'll call a Realtor and see what's available."

"People will wonder why you moved out. There'll be talk."

"There would be a lot more talk if I stay, don't you think?"

"Yes," was all she could say.

"If you need me—"

"I'll call."

He let himself out quickly and quietly, leaving Susan alone. She wanted to run after him, to call him back, to beg him not to leave her. But she didn't move. Not a muscle. She barely breathed.

It'll be better this way, she told herself. You'll see. It'll be so much easier when he's gone.

Six

"**D**id you put the kittens in the pet carrier for Mr. Heffernan?" Susan asked. "He's going to pick them up at ten-thirty this morning."

"They're all ready to go." Resting his forearm atop the broom he held, Scooter Bellamy looked at Susan through the thick lenses of his black-framed glasses. "Mr. Heffernan's got a big farm, doesn't he? And a great big old barn where the kittens can stay when it's cold or rainy."

"That's right," Susan assured him. "You know I wouldn't let the kittens go to anyone who wasn't going to be good to them."

"Of course I know that," Scooter said in his slow, slightly slurred speech. "Oh, yeah, I done give the cocker-lab mutt a bath, so he'll be all bright and shiny when that little girl comes and gets him today."

"Thanks, Scooter. That mutt is Carrie Johnson's birthday present. Her mom's bringing her by around noon, right before her birthday party."

Susan felt fortunate to have Scooter working as her assistant at the animal shelter. Folks said he wasn't very smart, and a few even made fun of him. But Susan loved the learning impaired man because he had one of the biggest hearts in the world. And he loved animals as much, if not more, than she did. Scooter was nearly forty, had never been married and still lived at home with his widowed mother.

"I'm going to be in the office for a while," Susan told him. "I have a lot of paperwork to catch up on."

"I'll stop by and we'll have coffee together at tenthirty." Scooter tapped the face of his Mickey Mouse watch and grinned a toothy, lopsided smile.

"I'll have the coffee ready." Susan returned his smile, then headed for the small room at the front of the shelter that she had redecorated when she'd taken over the job as manager ten years ago.

Susan opened the shutters to allow the morning sunshine to warm her office. She made preparations for the coffee and set the timer on the machine so that she and Scooter would have a freshly brewed pot for their morning break. After hanging her camel-colored wool coat and beige hat on the oak coatrack by the door, she sat down at her desk, lifted a stack of correspondence out of a top drawer and placed it on the blotter in front of her. She needed to get these letters written and mailed today! She'd been so busy making plans for the Christmas Open House at the shelter, she'd let other matters slide. But the open house had become a yearly event, and in the past they'd often been able to give away up to half their residents as Christmas presents for families who wanted pets.

She thanked God that she had something to keep her busy, something to occupy her mind—something other than Hank Bishop. Even though they'd shared Thanksgiving dinner together with the Bishop family at the governor's

mansion in Nashville—everyone except the elusive Jake—
Hank had kept his distance from her since the incident in
her kitchen nearly two weeks ago. He called her every day
instead of stopping by to check on her. She told herself that
she should be thankful that he wasn't pursuing her because
she honestly didn't know how long she'd be able to hold
out against him if he did.

She often stood at the back door and watched him leave
for work in the mornings, but she was usually in bed when
he returned at night. She didn't know where he went or
with whom he spent his evenings, and she had purposely
avoided asking Sheila or Donna if they'd heard anything
about his dating.

He hadn't called her today. Not yet. But she knew he
would. He never missed a day. Yesterday he'd told her that
the Realtor had finally found him an apartment, but he
wouldn't be moving until the first of January. After that,
even her daily glimpse of him from afar would come to an
end.

Just as Susan removed the rubber band from around the
stack of letters, a soft rap sounded at the door.

"Please, come in," she said.

The door opened and Donna Fields, draped in a purple
calf-length coat, breezed into the office, dropped her purple
leather bag on Susan's desk and unbuttoned her coat. "Do
you have a few minutes?" Donna asked. "I really need to
talk to you." She hung her coat beside Susan's on the rack,
then turned around and let out a long sigh.

"Sure. I can make time," Susan said as she stood and
walked around the desk. "Is something wrong?" She motioned to the leather sofa. "Do you want to sit down?"

"No, thanks," Donna said, and paced around the office,
her purple heels tapping against the wooden floor. "You're
my first stop and then I'm headed over to the garage to see
Sheila."

Susan grabbed Donna's arm, halting her frantic movements. "What on earth's the matter with you?" Never had she seen her cool, sophisticated friend so nervous.

Donna placed her hand over Susan's and patted her, then smiled sadly. "Remember this past August when Joanie Richardson and I took that three week archaeology tour out West and I stayed over a few extra days?"

"Yes." Susan stared quizzically at her elegant friend, a woman whose innate good taste and pedigree lineage Susan greatly envied.

"Well, I met a man. A very interesting man. I stayed over to be with him."

"You did?" Susan smiled, delighted that Donna had finally found someone who'd made her forget her devotion to her late husband's memory. "That's wonderful."

"It was wonderful. For a short time. We—we got married—"

Susan gasped loudly. "You what? When?"

"We got married in August. A whirlwind kind of thing. But after a few days, I realized I'd made a terrible mistake and…well, I came home and we had the marriage annulled."

"I see." But Susan didn't understand at all. Why was Donna telling her about this now? Why not months ago? "I'm sorry it didn't work out for you."

"The thing is…you see…I'm pregnant."

"You're pregnant?"

"Four months pregnant and I'm going to be showing soon, so I have to be prepared for a great many questions from friends, acquaintances and colleagues."

"Does he know? Your husband, er, that is…" Susan noted Donna's flushed cheeks and downcast eyes. Donna didn't blush. And she never avoided direct eye contact. Something was wrong here.

"No, he doesn't know, and I don't intend to contact him. I never want to see the man again as long as I live."

"You don't want to see him again, but you want to have his baby."

Donna stared, openmouthed, at Susan. "I...well, I... This is my baby. I don't think of it as his."

"What's his name?" Susan asked, beginning to figure out what was wrong with Donna's scenario.

"His name?"

"Yes, his name. You know...John Smith, Jimmy Brown, or maybe it was Bill Jones."

Donna slumped down on the sofa, sighed dejectedly and said, "You know, don't you?"

"Whoever fathered your baby was never your husband, not even briefly. And my guess is you don't even know his name."

"I know his name!" Donna said indignantly. "It was J.B."

"J.B. what?"

Donna buried her face in her hands. "I don't know. Just J.B."

Susan sat beside Donna and wrapped her arm comfortingly around her friend's shoulders. "You had a fling out in New Mexico with a guy named J.B. and now you're pregnant and have to come up with some sort of explanation that the locals might believe. Is that it?"

"Yes, that's it." Donna looked directly at Susan. "But if I couldn't convince you, how will I ever be able to convince anyone else. You're the most trusting person I know. So if you didn't believe me—"

"Sheila and I will help you perpetuate this myth of yours," Susan said. "We'll claim that you told us all about it just as soon as you came home from your trip last August."

"Thank goodness I have friends who are willing to lie

for me.'' Donna paused briefly, blushed again and said, ''He...that is, J.B. took precautions. We didn't have unprotected sex. I suppose one of the condoms was defective or... Oh, God, Susan, I've never done anything so foolish in my entire life! Ron was my only lover and I was a virgin when I married him.''

''You really want this child, don't you?''

''Yes, I do,'' Donna admitted. ''Despite the circumstances of my baby's conception, I want her or him very much. I know you can't begin to understand. You're so lucky that the child you're carrying is Lowell's. You won't have to figure out how someday you're going to explain why your child has no father and you can't even give her or him the man's name.''

''Oh, Donna, if you only knew.'' Susan sighed.

''What do you mean, *if I only knew?*''

''You aren't the only one who did something foolish and is now reaping the consequences.''

''What are you talking about?'' Donna asked.

''No one else knows,'' Susan said. ''Besides the doctors, that is. Only Sheila and Caleb.''

''Only Sheila and Caleb know what?''

''Lowell was sterile. This baby—'' Susan laid her hand over her tummy ''—was conceived by artificial insemination.''

Donna gasped. ''You're kidding me? Are you saying that you agreed to be impregnated with sperm from some anonymous donor?''

''Not exactly.''

''You know who the donor is?''

''Yes.'' Susan realized that she should have shared this information with Donna when she'd confided in Sheila, but she and Sheila had been friends since childhood and she'd thought it wise that as few people as possible know the truth. "Lowell asked Hank Bishop to...donate...his sperm."

"Hank Bishop! Oh, my God! Hank Bishop, who's living in your garage apartment? Hank Bishop whom you once had a mad crush on when you were a teenager?"

"Yes, that Hank Bishop."

Donna giggled. Once. Twice. And then she burst into full-fledged laughter. She laughed until tears streamed down her cheeks. For a couple of minutes Susan sat there and stared at her friend in a she's-lost-her-mind way, then suddenly Susan, too, burst into laughter.

And that's how Sheila Bishop found them when she flew into Susan's office. Susan wiped the tears from her eyes and smiled at Sheila, but one look at Sheila's solemn face told Susan that something was terribly wrong.

"What's wrong?" Susan asked. "What's happened?"

"It's Hank," Sheila said. "He and his deputies captured Carl Bates this morning. Bates had come back to Marshall County and was hiding in a shack out in Kingsley Woods. He didn't surrender without a struggle. There was a gun-fight and—"

Susan jumped up off the sofa, grabbed Sheila by the shoulders and demanded, "What happened? Is Hank all right?"

"He was shot," Sheila said.

"Oh, dear Lord," Susan cried as the painful reality struck her. "Is he...is he—"

"He's alive. That's all I know. They took him straight to County General. The minute we got word, Caleb left straight for the hospital and I came to get you."

"He can't die," Susan said. "I can't lose Hank, too."

Deputy Holman met them at the emergency room door. Susan thought he looked like a man who'd been to hell and back. His uniform was stained with dried blood. His hair was disheveled and his face lined with worry.

"Caleb asked me to wait down here for y'all," Richard Holman said.

"Where's Hank?" Susan demanded as she rushed past Sheila and Donna.

"He's in surgery, Mrs. Redman," Richard explained. "Caleb's upstairs in the waiting room. Come with me and I'll take y'all straight on up."

The three women fell into step alongside the deputy as he made his way to the elevators.

"How seriously was Hank wounded?" Susan asked as the elevator doors closed behind them.

"He took a bullet in the side," Richard said. "One of his lungs collapsed."

"Oh, no." Susan crumpled as her legs weakened.

Sheila and Donna, who flanked Susan, grabbed her by the elbows and kept her on her feet. Sheila gave the deputy a censoring glare.

Richard cleared his throat and said, "But the doctors say he'll be just fine. Honest to Pete, Mrs. Redman. You don't have to worry about Sheriff Bishop."

Susan willed herself to be strong. She hadn't fallen apart when Lowell was killed and she wasn't going to come to pieces now. Hank wasn't dead. He had been shot, was undergoing surgery and would come through just fine. Surely the good Lord wouldn't take away both of the men she loved. Not Lowell *and* Hank. No compassionate God could be that cruel, could He?

The minute they reached the waiting room, Caleb Bishop stopped pacing, turned and opened his arms to Susan. She went gladly into his comforting embrace.

"He's going to be okay," Caleb said. "I talked to him for a minute before they wheeled him out of ER and up to surgery."

"He was conscious when they brought him in?" Susan asked, pulling out of Caleb's arms.

"Oh, he was conscious, all right," Caleb said. "I thought the doctor in the ER was going to have to knock him out to work on him."

Susan smiled, remembering how bossy and take-charge Hank had always had been. "I suppose he thought he knew more than the doctor."

Caleb chuckled. "Partly. But mostly he was worried about you, about how you'd react when you found out he'd been shot. He kept telling me to make sure you didn't get too upset."

Susan glanced meaningfully at Deputy Holman. Caleb nodded his understanding.

"You know how protective Hank is of you, your being Lowell's widow and all," Caleb said. "He was concerned about the baby."

Tears filled Susan's eyes. Caleb led her over to a vinyl sofa in the corner. When she sat, Sheila and Donna closed in ranks to sit on either side of her.

"Have you had a chance to call Tallie?" Sheila asked.

"Yeah, I put in a call to her a few minutes ago," Caleb said. "She and Peyt should be here in a couple of hours."

Time passed slowly, agonizingly. Seconds turned to minutes and minutes to hours. Tallie and her husband, Governor Peyton Rand, arrived and joined the vigil. Richard's wife, an R.N. at the hospital, stopped by frequently, as did Kendra Camp, who worked upstairs in the obstetrical ward. Sheriff's deputies and city policemen trickled in and out, concerned about Hank. Businessmen and farmers, friends and acquaintances called to check on the progress of Hank's surgery. Susan's neighbors, Mrs. Dobson and Mrs. Brown, brought in sandwiches and coffee and offered their prayers. The whole county was breathing a collective sigh of relief that Carl Bates had finally been apprehended and was behind bars. And every citizen of Crooked Oak and the surrounding towns knew who they could thank for capturing the man who had killed Lowell Redman.

"The Bishop family?" the doctor in green scrubs inquired as he halted outside the waiting room.

Everyone jumped, almost in unison. Caleb walked over to the doctor, Tallie fast on his heels. Susan stood slowly, walked across the room and waited behind Hank's siblings.

"Hank came through surgery just fine," Dr. Hall said, and went on to explain Hank's condition quite succinctly. "He's in SICU, but I expect we'll move him into a private room by tonight. If there are no complications—and I don't expect any—he should be able to go home by the end of the week."

"When can we see him?" Caleb asked.

"A couple of family members can go in and see him in a few minutes," Dr. Hall said, then disappeared down the hallway.

"I'll feel a lot better when I see for myself that he's alive," Tallie said, then hugged Caleb.

Caleb glanced at Susan and said, "I think you should go in with Tallie and see Hank."

"No, that's all right—" Susan said.

Tallie glanced back and forth from Caleb to Susan, her eyes questioning. A look of annoyance wrinkled her forehead. "What's going on? What don't I know?"

"Nothing, smarty-pants," Caleb said. "Absolutely nothing."

"Caleb knows how much I've come to rely on Hank since Lowell died," Susan offered as an explanation. "He was just being considerate offering to let me go in and see Hank first."

Sheila and Donna eased gradually closer and closer to Susan and she noticed her two friends exchange a questioning glance. Great. Just great. No doubt Sheila had just realized Donna knew that Hank had fathered Susan's baby. She decided that it was unfair to continue keeping the truth from Tallie. After all, Hank's baby sister had been her friend as long as Sheila had.

When Tallie grabbed Susan's arm and pulled her off into a corner, Donna and Sheila followed.

"What's going on between you and Hank?" Tallie asked. "And don't try to tell me nothing. Remember I was around when we were teenagers. I know what a crush you had on Hank. You didn't hide your feelings for him quite as well as Sheila hid her feelings for Caleb."

Quietly and calmly, Susan explained the whys and wherefores of her baby's conception to Tallie. No one said a word until Susan finished speaking, and then Tallie groaned loudly.

"What the hell were you thinking?" Tallie spoke quietly but firmly. "What was Hank thinking? You're pregnant with my brother's baby. And we all know that the big lug is scared senseless of becoming a father. Hank remembers what things were like with our irresponsible father and although he is the most honorable, responsible man on earth, he's always been afraid that poor parenting is hereditary."

"As far as the world knows, this baby is Lowell's," Susan said. "Hank will be my child's godfather and that's all."

"Oh, yeah, sure." Tallie rolled her eyes heavenward. "Tell that to somebody who doesn't know Hank the way I do."

"Will you lighten up?" Donna slipped her arm around Susan's shoulders. "Don't you think Susan's been through enough without you trying to make her feel guilty?"

"I'm not trying to make her feel guilty," Tallie said. "I'm just trying to—"

"Then you should sound a little more supportive and a little less critical," Sheila suggested.

"I'm not being—" Tallie began, then was interrupted by her brother.

"Tallie, you and Susan can go in and see Hank now," Caleb said.

"What?" Tallie rushed toward the door, then stopped abruptly and glanced back over her shoulder at Susan. "Well, come on. Let's go."

Five minutes later when Susan stood at an unconscious Hank's bedside, her eyes swimming in tears as she held his limp hand, Tallie grabbed her other hand and squeezed it.

"You're still crazy about him, aren't you?" Tallie whispered.

"Yes," Susan said softly.

That night around eight, when Hank was moved into a private room, the whole family circled his bed as he came to groggily.

"I told this bunch of weeping females that you were too mean and ornery to die," Caleb said.

"How about some water?" Hank asked.

Everyone in the room made a move toward the water pitcher on the beside table, but one by one, they halted and watched as Susan lifted the plastic jug, poured the water into a matching aqua-green glass and inserted a straw. She held the glass with one hand and put the straw to his lips with the other. He sipped the liquid slowly, all the while watching Susan closely.

"Thanks," he said after he'd drunk all he wanted.

Susan made no move to leave his side and no one tried to usurp her position. "I—we were very worried about you."

"I'm fine, honey." He glanced around the room at the others, each with their eyes diverted from Susan and him, and he realized that sometime between yesterday and today someone had told Tallie and Peyton and Donna Fields the truth about Susan's baby. It was there in all their faces, in the way they couldn't bring themselves to look directly at him. Obviously, everyone was aware of the bond between him and Susan—the bond that went beyond the fact that she was carrying his child. These were their friends and family, the people who knew them best, and they'd all made an unanimous judgment call. They all knew just how much he cared about Lowell's widow. And apparently Susan wasn't able to hide her feelings for him, either.

"No one outside this room ever needs to know the truth," Hank said. "That's the way Susan and I want to handle the situation. As far as anyone else knows or will ever know, the child Susan is carrying belongs to Lowell."

Silence hung heavily in the room, like a thick, anesthetic fog that had rendered everyone speechless. Caleb pulled up a chair alongside Hank's bed, then gave Susan a gentle nudge. She didn't protest in the least.

After she sat, she glanced around at the somber faces and said, "Hank and I don't ask for your approval, but we do ask for your support."

Hank lifted his left hand, the one not connected to a tube, and reached up toward Susan. She clasped his hand in hers.

He tried to squeeze her hand, but he didn't have the strength to do more than weakly grasp it. His head hurt. His side ached. And he was feeling a little sick to his stomach. The last thing he wanted was a confrontation with anyone, least of all his own family. He knew that Tallie probably felt just the way Caleb did—that if he didn't claim his child, he would live to regret it.

"I think it's time we all left and let Hank get some rest," Peyton Rand said. "We shouldn't forget that he was shot less than twelve hours ago."

"Peyt's right," Caleb agreed. "Let's clear out. We can all come back tomorrow."

"I'll be back tomorrow," Tallie said. "And sooner or

later, Hank Bishop, you and I are going to have ourselves a little talk.''

''I never doubted that for a minute,'' Hank told his sister. ''I didn't expect you'd let me off the hook that easily.''

''Come on, Susan,'' Sheila said. ''I'll take you and Donna back to the animal shelter to pick up your cars.''

''You go on,'' Susan said. ''Take Donna. I'm going to stay.''

''No, you're not!'' Releasing Susan's hand, Hank glared up at her. ''I don't need for you to stay. I've got a hospital full of nurses at my beck and call. You should go home and rest.''

Susan looked directly at Sheila. ''Go ahead. I can call a cab, if I decide to go home before morning.''

Sheila nodded agreement and she and Donna left without saying another word.

Susan snapped her head around and said, ''You're in no condition to make me leave, so just shut up! I'm staying.''

''Why the hell won't you leave?''

''Because... Please, Hank, don't ask me to go.''

''I don't need you. Go home.''

''No, I'm staying.''

He clenched his jaw tightly. Damn stubborn woman. Didn't she realize that if she stayed at his side all night long, people were bound to notice? ''Why do you want to stay when I don't want you here?''

''Because...I can't leave you.'' She spoke the words so softly, so quietly, that for just a second he thought he hadn't heard her correctly. But when he looked up into her misty eyes, he knew that he had. Damn, how did she do it? How the hell did she turn him inside out this way?

''If you're determined to stay, ask the nurse to have a cot set up for you,'' he said tersely. ''You're pregnant, for God's sake, you don't need to be sitting up in a chair all night.''

She batted away the tears that escaped her eyes and then smiled at him. "All right. I'll go ask for a cot." She got up, walked across the room and paused just before she opened the door. "Oh, and one other thing—for your information, Mr. Bishop, I don't care who notices that I'm concerned enough about you to spend the night here." Without a backward glance, she left the room.

Seven

Everyone Hank knew in Marshall County thought Susan's devotion to him was admirable. The way she stayed at his side the night after he'd been shot. The way she came by the hospital morning, noon and night to check on him. The way she had insisted that he come home with her so she could personally take care of him while he recuperated. He'd even overheard a couple of hospital volunteers discussing their take on the situation.

"You know she couldn't look after Lowell, nurse him back to health and all. Poor girl, she's doing for her husband's best friend what she couldn't do for her husband," one lady said.

"So sad—isn't it?—that she lost her husband while she was just barely a month along in her pregnancy," the other lady said. "And then she almost lost the man who stepped in to fill Lowell's shoes. What would that sweet girl do without Hank Bishop to see her through these next few months?"

No one, except for his family, seemed to suspect that there was anything between Susan and him. Nothing more than the bond formed by their mutual love for Lowell Redman. And of course, that bond was in and of itself a very strong one. And so was the bond created by the child she carried. But what truly united them and yet at the same time kept them at arm's length was mutual desire. He could not—would not—make a move on Susan, knowing how vulnerable she was. He wasn't the kind of man who took advantage of women. Least of all a woman who deserved nothing less than a lifetime commitment.

With a cold beer in one hand and the remote control in the other, Hank sat in the overstuffed chair in his living room, watching a program about hunting on one of the local stations. He'd been home from the hospital three days and he was bored out of his skull. His side still ached some. The incision itched. And his head throbbed. Everybody from one end of town to the other had called him this morning. Checking on him. Concerned. Caring. He'd finally unplugged the phone, after Susan had called for the fourth time today. Why the hell couldn't she just leave him alone?

His family had been at Susan's to welcome him home three days ago, and Tallie had even threatened to take him back to Nashville with her if he didn't behave himself. He'd had to fight the whole damn bunch for the right to come back to his apartment alone. Susan had practically pleaded with him to stay in her home and allow her to play nursemaid. The last thing he needed was Susan hovering around him, looking at him with those big blue eyes, touching him with those soft hands. The two of them under the same roof would be tempting fate. And he wasn't a guy who took unnecessary chances when he knew the odds were against him.

If he could survive until Tuesday, then he could go back to work and end the boredom. And after Christmas, he'd move into his new apartment. Maybe seven miles separating him and Susan would be enough to quell his desire for her. He couldn't go on seeing her every day without betraying Lowell's memory, without betraying Susan's trust and without betraying his own principles.

The soft rap on the door was barely audible over the television, and he tried to ignore the sound. He figured it was Susan. Again. She'd brought his lunch over on a tray, then had come back an hour later and retrieved the tray. No doubt she was here now with his dinner. These mealtime visits had become routine since his return from the hospital.

The knocking grew louder. He grunted. Go away and leave me alone! He wanted to shout at her, to warn her to stay the hell away from him. But she wouldn't leave him alone. She wouldn't stay away. Her constant attention was driving him up the wall. Couldn't she understand that he didn't want her sympathy, her concern, her damn chicken potpies! He wanted *her*. Naked. In his arms. Moaning his name as he buried himself deeply within her.

"Hank? Hank, are you all right?" Susan called through the closed door. "Please, Hank, answer me."

He shot up out of the chair. A sharp pain sliced through his right temple. He groaned inwardly as he stormed to the door, swung it open and glared at Susan.

"Hi," she said in that soft, sexy little voice that made his whole body tense with awareness of her. "I've brought your supper. Pork chops. Scalloped potatoes. Butter beans. Corn muffins. And lemon icebox pie." She held a large tray, covered with a striped cloth.

"Susan, you don't have to do this, you know. Keep fixing my meals." He leaned casually against the door frame, bracing himself with one hand. "You have to be running yourself ragged trying to work every day and take care of me, too. I'm just fine. You can stop worrying about me."

She nudged his chest gently with the tray. "You need to eat this while it's still hot."

He eased aside and allowed her entrance. She swept past him, across the room and to the small dining table in the corner, near the one side window. She placed the tray on the table, whipped off the protective cloth and pulled out the chair.

"Sit down and eat. I'll put on a pot of coffee," she told him.

He grabbed her wrist as she reached up into the cabinet toward the pack of coffee filters. She turned and smiled at him.

"I can fix coffee, if I want it," he said. "And I'm perfectly capable of fixing myself a sandwich or opening a can of soup or zapping a frozen dinner in the microwave."

"Of course you are." She stroked his cheek with her free hand. "But I have to cook for myself anyway, so it's no trouble to fix enough for two."

His jaw tensed when she touched him. Why did she have to touch him? Didn't she know what that did to him? "Susan, I don't want you to keep bringing me my lunch and dinner every day. Do you understand?"

"No, I'm afraid I don't understand." The smile faded from her lips. She glanced down at her wrist manacled in his big hand. "What are you trying to tell me?"

He released his hold on her wrist and stepped back, putting a couple of feet between their bodies. "I'm saying that I don't want you going to so much trouble to—"

"And I just told you that it's no trouble. It's my pleasure."

She was looking at him, all soft and feminine and tempting. The subtle approach wasn't going to work with Susan. Why was she doing this to him? Why couldn't she just walk away and leave well enough alone?

Frustration overrode his common sense. He grabbed her

shoulders and shook her a couple of times—gently, but with enough force to get her attention. "I'm sick and tired of your hovering around me, showering me with all this T.L.C. I'm not your husband. I'm not your lover. I might have taken over Lowell's job—temporarily—but I'm not taking over his role as the man in your life."

"I—I never thought that you were taking—"

"If you think showing me what a loving, attentive little wife you can be is going to make me want to stick around and be the kind of husband Lowell was, the kind of father he would have been, then think again, honey. I don't want to take Lowell's place as your husband. And I never wanted to be a father."

She glowered at him for a second, then reached out and slapped his face soundly. Tears welled up in her eyes. She sucked in a deep, agonized breath, then turned and ran.

Hank stood there, stunned by her physical attack. He rubbed his stinging cheek. All right. So maybe he'd been a little too brutal. But it had been her fault, not his, that he'd had to be so blunt.

He stared at the open door. Listened to her footsteps as she dashed down the wooden stairs.

Don't go after her, you idiot. Don't you dare run after her!

He rushed out onto the stoop at the top of the stairs. "Susan!"

She slammed the back door when she entered her house.

"Susan, dammit!"

He raced down the stairs, across the yard and up onto the back porch. Lifting his hand, he started to knock on the door, but thought better of the idea and reached for the doorknob. Surprisingly, it turned and the door opened. She hadn't locked the door. She'd been too angry and hurt to think rationally, he told himself as he entered the kitchen.

"Susan, honey, where are you? We need to talk."

Fred and Ricky met him in the hallway, both mutts yapping at his heels. In the corner Lucy eyed him as if he were a trapped mouse, and from behind him, he heard the hiss of Ethel's breath. Great! That's all he needed—to have Susan's animal entourage attack him.

"Susan? I'm sorry. Okay?"

No response.

"I had no right to say those things to you. I *am* sorry."

Hank searched the downstairs, but didn't find her. Where the hell was she? He climbed the stairs, two growling dogs and two evil-eyed cats following him. He opened the first door he came to and found the small room empty, except for buckets of unopened paint and rolls of wallpaper and border lying on the floor. Suddenly he realized that he'd stumbled into the room Susan was planning to use for a nursery. He exited quickly and went down the hall to the next room. The door stood wide open, revealing a large bedroom that he instantly knew must have once belonged to Miss Alice. An enormous, ornately carved antique bed dominated the room, which apparently was, as was the room next to it, being redecorated.

Susan lay across the bed, her shoulders trembling as she sobbed quietly. How was he going to handle this situation? He hadn't wanted to hurt her, hadn't wanted to make her cry. But what choice had she given him?

"Susan?" He called her name from the doorway.

She lifted her head a fraction, glanced over her shoulder and stared at him, her eyes red, her cheeks flushed and damp with tears. A hard knot formed in the pit of his stomach. He didn't think he'd ever made a woman cry. He deliberately avoided circumstances that would create this type of emotional display.

"What are you doing here?" she asked, gasping between sobs.

"I came to apologize," he told her as he took a tentative step into the room.

Susan's snarling mutts followed him. The two cats crawled up on the bed, flanking their mistress in a protective manner. He didn't like the idea that her animals thought they had to guard her against him. He wasn't going to hurt her. *No, you dope,* his conscience reminded him, *you've already done that, haven't you? You've already hurt her.*

I was just trying to save both of us some major grief, he told himself silently, hoping she would understand without his explaining any further about how dangerous they were to each other.

"You don't have to apologize." She sat up on the side of the bed and looked directly at him. "I didn't realize what you thought...how you felt. I never meant to crowd you. I don't expect anything from you, Hank. I know you didn't volunteer to take Lowell's place as a husband and father."

"I shouldn't have said that." Hank took a few more hesitant steps toward the bed.

"Yes, you should have. You had every right to say exactly what you meant. I'm the one who...I overreacted." She stood, her movements slow and cautious.

"You've got to know what this is really all about." He closed the distance between them quickly, halting when only a couple of feet separated them. "I'm not husband and father material, honey. So if that's what you're looking for, then you've got the wrong man."

"I know." She reached out, her hand trembling, and caressed his cheek. "Of course, I know what this is all about. It's about the fact that I'm Lowell's widow and you're his best friend and it's wrong for us to want each other. But...we do."

"Yeah, we do, don't we?" His heartbeat roared in his

ears like a jet engine. His sex hardened and throbbed. His head told him to run. His body demanded that he stay.

She draped her arms around his neck, stood on tiptoe and brought her lips to his. "The way you make me feel scares me. It always has. I've been running from these feelings since I was a teenager. I'm tired of running. Tired of trying to pretend that I don't want you so much that the wanting is ripping me apart inside."

"No promises," he said, his voice husky with emotion. "No commitment. Just this moment and what we're feeling now."

"Yes." With that one word, Susan surrendered to Hank and to the wild, untamed emotions that she had kept buried deep inside her all her life.

He wrapped her in his arms, lowered his head and took her mouth. Sweet heaven! The feel of her pressing against him was his undoing. She clung to him, making soft, little feminine sounds deep in her throat as he plunged in his tongue and explored the warmth inside her. She responded instantly, fervently, enticing his tongue in an age-old mating dance. He moved his hands down her back, over her hips and around to cup her buttocks and bring her mound intimately against his sex. He pulsed against her. She rubbed rhythmically against him.

He backed her up against the edge of the bed. She swayed. He eased her onto the bed, his body following hers. He poised himself on his elbows, hovering over her, his gaze feasting on the sight of her—small, vulnerable, and totally helpless—lying beneath him.

"If you don't want this, tell me now." He growled the words, as if saying them pained him greatly.

This was her most treasured fantasy—and her most terrifying nightmare. Surrendering to her wanton desire for Hank. He was giving her this one final chance to escape. She could tell that he was holding on to his iron will, that he was still in control, but just barely. He was a man on the precipice, ready to plunge headlong into the abyss. And he would take her with him, down into that hot, sultry darkness—unless she told him no. And told him now.

"I want this," she said. "It's what I've always wanted. You, Hank. You."

Her words seemed to free something inside him. Not that it was a visible thing, Susan thought. It was more of a feeling she sensed.

Lowering his head, he covered her lips and kissed her passionately. Her stomach fluttered, her toes curled and her femininity clenched and unclenched in preparation. He ended the kiss, then lifted himself up and off the bed. With quick precision, he divested himself of his shirt and flung it to the floor.

She sucked in a deep breath, her nerves singing, her body yearning, as she looked at his naked chest. Broad, muscled and hairy. And marred by a small, healing scar across the left side of his rib cage. His shoulders looked massive, his arms huge. He was, without a doubt, the most beautiful man she'd ever seen. Her man. The man of her dreams.

How many women never got a chance like this? How many spent their whole lives without ever knowing the joy of being with the one man on earth meant for them?

He knelt over her, reached down and lifted her into a sitting position. She allowed him to have his way with her. He pulled her beige cashmere sweater up her body and over her head, then tossed it on top of his shirt.

Her breathing quickened, lifting and lowering her breasts. Hank unlatched the front hook of her satin bra and spread it apart, exposing her to his heated gaze. Her nipples tightened under his scrutiny.

"Sweet heaven," he moaned.

His mouth covered one breast. His tongue laved the nipple. She felt herself unraveling when his thumb stroked her other nipple. Warmth spread through her, rapidly raising her temperature, and moisture pooled at the apex between her thighs.

Hank kissed her belly, then lifted her hips enough to reach under her and tug the elastic waistband of her slacks down and over her legs and off over her ankles, taking her beige leather flats off in the process. Returning to her as soon as he removed her cream-colored knee-highs, he delved his hand inside her silk panties. His fingers sought and found her core. He stroked her intimately, eliciting a cry of astonished pleasure from her before he inserted two fingers inside her, as if testing her readiness.

"You're so hot and wet, honey." He lowered her panties, discarded them and then buried his face in the tawny brown thatch between her legs.

He eased her onto her back, spread her legs and painted a damp trail up one inner thigh and down the other. Susan shivered uncontrollably. She had never known anything so incredibly sensual, so wantonly delicious. He touched and tormented her breasts and her feminine core. His fingers pinched and probed and teased with indescribable pleasure. His lips and tongue kissed and licked and sucked until she was mindless with sensation—hot, wild, sexual feelings unlike anything she'd felt before this night. Before this man.

She clutched at the bedspread beneath her, wadding the material in her hands as her hips lifted and she gave herself over to complete and utter abandonment. Her body jerked with release. Hank intensified his actions, pushing her farther and farther, deeper and deeper into pure, sweet ecstasy. When she lay spent, her breathing ragged, her body flushed, he lifted himself up and over her.

She looked into his dark eyes—searing black eyes that told her of his intentions. He kicked off his shoes and slipped out of his socks. In one swift move, he unsnapped and unzipped his jeans, then removed them and his briefs. And suddenly, he was over her, on her, entering her.

He lifted her hips as he plunged into her, bringing their bodies together completely. When he was buried deep inside her, he paused and waited for her to adjust to his size.

She felt full, expanded to the limits and nothing had ever been so right, so powerfully, undeniably right. She touched him. Caressed his chest. His tight, little male nipples. She curled her fingers in his chest hair. And then she ran her hands over his broad shoulders, loving the feel of his strength beneath her fingertips.

He withdrew from her. Moaning, she clung to him. He lunged again, deeply, completely, and she cried out from the sheer joy of having him inside her. The primitive rhythm began, slowly, gently, and then soon the pace accelerated until the beat of their mating grew faster and faster, harder and harder, wilder and wilder. They thrashed about on the bed, their bodies joined. He flipped her on top and she rode him frantically. Then he took the dominant position and brought them both to earth-shattering climaxes. Sweat glistened on their naked bodies as they melted into each other and fell, exhausted and sated, onto the bed.

When he ran the tips of his fingers over her stomach, she gasped and shivered. Aftershocks of fulfillment rippled through her. He lifted her in his arms, pulled down the covers, eased her back onto the bed and pulled her into his arms. She snuggled against him, praying this night would never end. He lifted the covers over them and draped his arm across her warm, damp body.

When he awoke, it was nearly midnight. Moonlight shimmered through the lace curtains at the long, narrow windows of the bedroom. He lifted himself up on one elbow and watched Susan as she slept. The soft moonlight illuminated the outline of her body, the rounded planes of her face. He smelled the womanliness of her sweet body, tinged with the heavier scent of his masculinity and overlaid with the earthy aroma of sex.

She moaned, then squirmed. The covers slipped off her breasts and down to her hips. He balled his hands into fists to control the desire to reach out and touch her, to caress those round full breasts, to stroke those tempting pink nipples. Her belly looked almost flat, except for the smallest little bulge. His hand hovered above that minute bulge and then, as if drawn by the child growing inside her, he laid his hand possessively—protectively—over her belly.

She mumbled in her sleep. His breath caught in his throat. How would he feel, he wondered, if she whispered Lowell's name?

But it wasn't Lowell's name on her lips that shocked him back to his senses. No, not Lowell's name, but his own.

"Hank." His name was a whispered murmur, spoken in the twilight between sleep and consciousness. "Oh, Hank. I love you."

Every nerve in his body screamed. His muscles tensed. This was what he'd feared the most, what he had wanted to avoid.

You should have known better. You should have known a woman like Susan wouldn't give herself to a man unless she loved him. You've done it now. You've made love to your best friend's widow and she thinks she's in love with you!

Hank eased out of bed and rummaged around on the floor, searching for his clothes. He didn't want to leave this way. Like a thief in the night. He wanted to stay, wake her and make love to her again and again and again. Once hadn't been enough. Not nearly enough. A dozen times, even ten dozen times wouldn't be enough to satisfy his hunger for Susan.

But she wasn't looking for a love affair. She wanted and needed a husband and a father for her unborn baby.

Your baby, some inner voice tormented him.

He slipped into his briefs and jeans, put on his shirt and picked up his shoes and socks. When he reached the door, he paused and glanced back at the woman lying in the bed. She had turned and snuggled up against his pillow. His sex hardened and he cursed his traitorous body for wanting a woman he had no right to claim.

She's carrying your child, he reminded himself once again. Doesn't that give you some sort of right to her? No! No, it didn't. If he was willing to marry her and claim the child as his, then, yes, that would give him definite rights. But he had no intention of doing either. He'd just screw up all three of their lives if he even considered the possibility.

The Bishop men had a lousy track record at fatherhood. Their grandfather had proven to be ill-equipped to raise them. Their own father had been irresponsible and a total failure at parenthood. And look at Caleb. Even though he was working hard at trying to make things up to Sheila and Danny now, he had gotten Sheila pregnant twelve years ago, left her and never once looked back. And Jake was probably the most irresponsible Bishop of them all. He had run away, not only from Crooked Oak, but from their family and any ties that bound them all together.

What right did he have to think he might do better at this family thing than his forebearers and his brothers? Tallie seemed to be the only Bishop that had gotten it right the first time. He had convinced himself long ago that marriage and fatherhood were not for him. He had no intention of bringing children into this world and screwing up their lives.

You're a little late for that now, aren't you? his conscience taunted him. *Susan is going to have your baby and that kid's going to grow up without a father. Lowell would have made a perfect dad for Susan's child. But not you. You'll probably even make a terrible godfather.*

If he thought he could give Susan what she and the baby deserved, he might stick around to try to make things work with her. But he didn't dare chance it.

He took one last look at Susan, turned and walked out into the hall. He eased quietly down the stairs, through the kitchen and out into the cold December night. Just before he started up the outside staircase leading to his apartment, he paused and looked back at Susan's house, up to the second floor windows of the bedroom where she slept.

"I'm sorry, honey," he whispered, his voice lost on the winter wind. An unbearable ache began deep inside him and he wondered if anything would ever ease the pain.

Susan lifted back the heavy lace curtain and watched as Hank trudged up the staircase to his apartment. His shirt was unbuttoned and he carried his belt and socks in his hands. He was running scared. Running from her and what had happened between them. She knew just how he felt. She'd been running scared all her life—running from the overwhelming passion and love she'd always felt for him.

Aunt Alice had been right about this kind of love—the wild, uninhibited, uncontrollable kind of desire that drove people mad. It was like a fever in the blood, consuming and conquering in its intensity. An addiction so powerful that it took precedence over everything and everyone in your life.

She had been Lowell's wife for two years. She had loved him, made love with him and shared his bed and his life. She had been content and satisfied with their marriage and the future they had planned together. But Lowell was gone. Her safe haven, her security, her beloved mate.

When Hank closed his apartment door behind him, Susan released the curtain and let it fall across the window, blocking out the sight of the garage. She sat down in the wing chair by the fireplace and curled her feet beneath her. Lucy jumped up on the back of the chair and Ethel perched on the arm. Fred and Ricky, resting side by side on the hearth rug, lifted their heads and looked up at her.

She sighed as she wrapped her arms around her waist. "What am I going to do?" Both cats stepped into her lap. The dogs ambled over to her feet. She sighed again as she stroked Lucy and Ethel and took turns rubbing Fred's and Ricky's tummies with her foot.

"I'm in love with him. I'm going to have his baby. And we just made love. But he's scared of making a commitment to me." She buried her face in her hands. "Oh, God, please help me. I love him more than anything on earth, but he doesn't love me. Aunt Alice was right. Love like this causes only pain in the long run."

Susan wept herself to sleep, curled in the big wing-back chair in her aunt's bedroom, her animals surrounding her protectively.

Eight

Susan heard Hank when he left his apartment the next morning. She stood at the kitchen door and watched him back his Jeep out of the driveway and onto the road in front of the house. Where was he going this early? He wasn't scheduled to return to work until Tuesday. When she had heard the Jeep's motor roar to life, she'd carried her glass of orange juice with her as she rushed to the door and looked out at the drive. She'd wanted to call out to him, to ask him why he wasn't coming over to see her this morning, why he was running away from her. And she knew that's what he was doing. He was running scared.

They had shared something exceedingly special last night, something so wonderful that just the memory of it created warmth and pleasure deep within her. Of course, the power of their joining, the strength of their feelings, had frightened her, too. But for the first time in her life, she wasn't trying to escape those intense emotions. She accepted the fact that she loved Hank Bishop—loved him with mindless abandon, with wild and tormenting passion. She wouldn't trade anything on earth for last night, for the experience of a lifetime.

Maybe Hank didn't love her. Or maybe he did and he just wasn't ready or able to make a commitment to her. The one thing she knew—knew for sure and certain—was that Hank had wanted her as much as she had wanted him. And their lovemaking had affected him as deeply and profoundly as it had affected her.

She would wait for him to return to his apartment. No matter where he'd gone, sooner or later, he had to return. And when he came back, she'd be waiting for him. If she had finally found the courage to face her greatest fears, then it was high time Hank faced his, too.

"I don't see why you couldn't come out to the farm for breakfast," Caleb grumbled as he laid his sheepskin-lined coat on the back of the booth at Dawn's Diner, a greasy spoon in downtown Crooked Oak.

"I didn't want to talk to you with Sheila around," Hank said, then glanced up at the skinny, blond waitress who appeared at his side. "Just coffee right now."

"Just two coffees?" she asked. "The booths are usually for folks eating breakfast. If y'all just want coffee, there's a couple of stools—"

"Give us both the Early Bird Special," Hank told her.

"Sure thing." She smacked her gum as she headed behind the counter and called out their breakfast order to the cook.

"So what's wrong?" Caleb asked. "You look like hell. Didn't you get any sleep last night? Is the gunshot wound giving you trouble?"

"The wound's healing up just fine. My problem is more serious." Hank glanced out the glass front wall of the diner, onto the street and sidewalk, both practically deserted at six o'clock in the morning.

"More serious than a gunshot wound? Must be woman trouble. So what's going on with you and Susan?"

Hank snapped his head around, lowered his voice and said, "Will you keep your voice down. I don't want half the town to overhear our conversation."

Caleb grunted. "Take a look at this place. We're the only customers, except for the two guys drinking coffee at the counter."

"I'm going to move into the apartment over on Grove Avenue, just as soon as I can, but I need a place to stay until then. I hate to ask you, but—"

"You know you're welcome to stay with us." Caleb smiled at the waitress when she sat two white mugs down on the table. "But why the rush to move? It's only a couple of weeks until the first."

Hank looked down at the table, eyed the coffee and lifted the mug. He blew on the steaming liquid, then took a sip. "I need to put some distance between Susan and me. And I need to do it today."

Caleb let out a long, low whistle. Hank gritted his teeth. The brothers looked directly at each other.

"I see," Caleb said. "Okay. Pack a bag and come on out to the farm whenever you're ready."

"Thanks."

"Are you going to talk to Susan, tell her where you're going?"

"Yeah, sure. I owe her that much."

"Just how serious is it between you two?" Caleb asked.

"Way too serious."

"Are you sure this is what you want to do? Maybe y'all could work it out, come to an agreement of some kind."

"No!"

"Mmm-hmm."

"I suppose Sheila will ask questions," Hank said.

"I'll ask her not to. But I'm sure she'll get Susan's version of what happened. You know, women like to talk about stuff."

Hell! That's all he needed—his sister-in-law being given an account of his love life by one of his lovers. But Susan wasn't just one of his lovers. And that was the problem. Susan was different. She was special.

The waitress set the plates filled with scrambled eggs, bacon, hash browns and grits on the table. Hank pulled a twenty out of his wallet, tossed it on top of his napkin and stood.

"I'll be on out to the farm in a few hours. Thanks."

He put on his coat as he walked out the door. He jumped into the Jeep, started the motor and then slammed his hands down on the steering wheel.

Fool! Damn fool! Why couldn't he have kept his hands off her? Why did he have to make love to her? If he needed a woman so damn bad, why hadn't he found somebody else…somebody who wouldn't get hurt…somebody who wouldn't have told him that she loved him?

Susan had gone into work early to catch up on things she'd let slide while Hank had been in the hospital. It seemed she'd let her whole life *slide* for the past several months. But her life hadn't been easy, either. First Lowell's murder. Then Hank Bishop's return to Crooked Oak. And most recently, Hank's gunfight with Carl Bates.

She glanced over the information from last year's springtime fund-raiser. Now that the mid-December Christmas Open House was behind her, it was past time she put the plans for the coming year's events into motion. April would be here soon enough.

And then May. And June. Her baby was due in June. Early June. She had planned to ask Hank to be her Lamaze coach. She hoped he'd want to be present when their baby was born.

But he's not going to claim the baby. He wants everyone to believe he's just the godfather.

Hadn't last night changed things for them—for him?

The minute she heard the knock at the door, her heart leaped up in her throat. She knew instinctively that it was Hank.

"Yes, please, come in," she said.

He opened the door a fraction, peered inside and waited. "I, uh…we need to talk. Have you got a few minutes?"

"Certainly." She shoved back her chair and rose to meet him. "Please, come on inside."

He entered her office, closed the door behind him and stood in front of her. For a couple of minutes, he stared down at the floor, then lifted his gaze and looked at her.

"I'm going out to stay with Caleb and Sheila until my new apartment is available."

"Oh."

"After what happened last night, I think…well, it would be better if we put a little distance between us."

This wasn't what she wanted, but it was what she had expected. "If you're sure it's for the best, then—"

"Last night was my fault. And I'm…"

Please, dear Lord, don't let him say that he's sorry.

"I'm feeling guilty for taking advantage of you the way I did. I wanted you," he said. "I still want you—" when she swayed toward him, he stepped back "—and that's the problem. It wouldn't be fair to you if we had an affair. When Lowell's term as sheriff is up, I'm going back to my job with the Bureau. You need to wait for a guy who wants to get married and be a father to…to your baby."

"Let me get this straight. You're doing all this for my own good? You're running off out to Caleb and Sheila's so you won't be tempted to make love to me again because you've decided that we shouldn't have an affair?''

"Yeah. That's about it."

"Don't I have a say in this?" she asked.

"What do you mean?"

"What if I don't want you to move? What if I want you to make love to me again? What if I'd like for us to have an affair?"

"You don't mean that. What would people say? You don't want people talking about you as if you were some, er, some—"

"Some wanton woman who doesn't give a tinker's damn what anyone thinks about her."

"Susan, honey, you're not yourself. You're not the kind of girl who has affairs. You're the kind who gets married."

She backed him up against the closed door, draped her arms around his neck and said, "First of all, Hank Bishop, I'm not a girl. I haven't been a girl in years. I'm a woman. And what I want—what I've always wanted—is you."

Hank pulled her arms from around his neck, but not before she kissed him. He sucked in a deep breath, reached behind him and opened the door.

"Lady, you're dangerous."

She watched him practically run out of her office. She didn't know whether to laugh or cry. The man she loved had just told her that he still wanted her—wanted her so badly that he didn't trust himself to continue living in close proximity to her.

Hank thought he didn't want to be a husband and a father, thought he'd be lousy at both. But somewhere deep down inside him, a man like Hank—honest, trustworthy, loyal, dependable—probably wanted those very things. And she knew, in her heart, that if Hank ever committed himself, he would be a faithful, loving husband and the best father in the world.

If she could overcome her fear of him—of the uncontrollable passion she'd always felt for him—then surely he could overcome his fear of commitment. Just because his father had been a lousy husband and father, didn't mean that he would be. Why couldn't he see that?

Hank tried to avoid her, but she took every chance possible to be around him. To remind him of the way he felt about her. To let him think about what he was missing. He didn't stop by the house to check on her, but he did call her daily. Short, succinct phone calls, without the least bit of familiarity in his side of the conversation. But she always made at least one personal comment that was sure to arouse him. She was actually getting very good at playing a telephone seductress.

The whole Bishop clan, short of the always missing Jake, shared Christmas at the farm. And they included her. Tallie had said, ''You've always been like a member of the family and now that you're carrying my little niece or nephew, that makes it official.'' Hank had gone out of his way not to get close to her during the holidays, despite the fact they were together for hours at a time. But she caught him staring at her, his gaze telling her that he still wanted her just as much as ever.

She was playing a waiting game, hoping and praying that in the end she would be the victor. But Hank was as stubborn as a mule. He had decided long ago—when he'd been a boy—that he was never going to get married and have kids.

The January wind whistled as it blew around the corner of Sophie's, the one Italian restaurant in Crooked Oak and by far the best in Marshall County. Susan and Donna hurried inside, stomping their feet on the giant rubber mat in the foyer. Dirty slush dropped from their shoes and fresh snow fell from their coats as they removed them and hung them on the long wall rack to their left.

"Table for two," Donna said, then glanced meaningfully at her protruding belly and then at Susan's slightly rounded tummy. "Definitely non-smoking."

The hostess showed them to a nice, cozy booth in the back of the restaurant. After sliding into the booth, they looked over the menus and when their waitress arrived, Donna ordered Veal Parmesan and Susan ordered the Spiced Chicken Salad.

"I'm glad we went to the movies tonight," Donna said. "I really needed to get out of the house and away from all my well-meaning friends who keep sticking their noses into my personal business. Even President Harper today asked me if there was no hope of a reconciliation between me and the baby's father."

"So, you think most people have bought your story about a whirlwind courtship and wedding and then an even quicker divorce?" Susan asked.

"I don't know," Donna admitted. "I think some people bought it and the ones who didn't are sympathetic enough not to question the validity of my very brief marriage."

"At least I had a husband," Susan said, then lowered her voice. "And no one would ever suspect that Lowell isn't my child's father."

"What if your child looks just like Hank Bishop?" Donna shook her head sadly. "We're a fine pair, aren't we? Two pregnant women with no fathers for their babies."

"I'm hoping my baby will have a father." Susan hushed immediately when the waitress brought their drinks and hot bread sticks.

"I thought you told me that Hank is steering clear of you these days."

"He is. But I haven't given up hope. I think once Hank

sees his child and holds him in his arms, he won't be able to walk away from us.''

"Him? You said him? Do you think the baby's a boy?''

"That's what they told me when I had the sonogram done today, and I've got the pictures to prove it.''

"I'm going to name my little girl, Louisa Christine, after my grandmothers.'' Donna glided her hand over her round tummy. "Think we should go ahead and arrange a marriage between your son and my daughter?''

Susan laughed. "I don't know how my son will feel about older women. After all, your Louisa will be a whole month older.''

"You know what's really funny about all this—about my being pregnant? Ron and I were married for four years and for two of those years, we tried to have a baby. It never happened. Two whole years of making love and nothing! Then I spend a couple of nights with a big, macho cowboy I hardly know and wham bam, I'm pregnant!''

"Donna, uh, have you ever thought about trying to contact this guy and tell him he's going to be a father? Maybe you two could—''

"I have no idea what his name is or how to reach him.''

"I'll bet you could find him if you wanted to. If other people in that bar knew his name was J.B., then maybe the bartender knew him and could—''

"He wasn't the kind of man I'd want to marry,'' Donna confessed. "He was rough and crude and I don't think he'd had much education, at least, he didn't talk like an educated man.''

"Do you realize how terribly snobbish you sound, Ms. Fields? And sexist, too. This man was good enough to sleep with, but not good enough to marry?''

"Oh, I know how it sounds. How it makes me look. But I swear, Susan, I've never done anything like that before in my life. It was as if I'd lost all my senses. You can't imagine how it feels to be so totally swept away by passion that you're powerless to stop yourself from making a terrible mistake.''

Susan grinned. ''That's where you're wrong. I know exactly what it feels like to be swept away by passion.''

''Are you saying that you and Hank...that y'all have...have—''

''Yes. Once. Before Christmas. That's why he moved out in such a hurry.''

They quieted instantly when the waitress brought the main course. Just as Susan lifted her fork, she glanced across the room to where the hostess was seating a new arrival. He had his back to her, but she'd know those broad shoulders, those lean hips, those long legs anywhere.

Her heartbeat accelerated. Her stomach quivered. Hank Bishop was only a few feet away from her. All she had to do was walk across the room and say hello. But she wouldn't do that. She still had some pride left. A week ago she had invited him to go with her to see the doctor today, to be there when they did the sonogram. He had declined the invitation. Then this afternoon, after her doctor's appointment, she had phoned him at his office.

''I have the sonogram pictures,'' she'd told him. ''The baby's perfect. If you'd like to see them or if you'd like to know whether the baby's a boy or a girl, you're welcome to stop by the house.''

He had declined that offer, too, so she'd been glad when Donna had called and suggested they go to the movies tonight. Neither of them felt like being alone.

''What are you staring at so hard?'' Donna turned and followed Susan's line of vision. ''Aha. Did you know Hank would be here tonight?''

''No. I knew he ate most of his meals out, but I didn't know he'd be eating at Sophie's tonight.''

''Want to ask him to join us?''

"I don't think so."

"He's looking this way," Donna said. "He's seen us. Smile and wave."

Susan and Donna smiled and waved. Hank did neither; he just nodded his head in recognition.

"He's eating alone," Donna said. "Wonder why he doesn't have a date?"

"He isn't dating," Susan replied. "Sheila told me that he hasn't had a date since that one date with Kendra Camp. And I understand that Kendra has called him several times, but he always finds an excuse not to see her."

"You're certainly keeping tabs on Sheriff Bishop, aren't you?"

Susan laid her hand over her small, round tummy. "I have a vested interest in Hank Bishop. My son and I."

Although it was delicious, Susan only nibbled at her dinner. Throughout the meal, she stole glances at Hank, who seemed to be having a difficult time concentrating on his food, too. And when the waitress flirted with him, he ignored her, but looked directly at Susan, as if checking to see if she would display some sign of jealousy. She didn't. She just smiled at him. Frowning, he glanced away and lifted his coffee cup.

After splitting the check, Susan and Donna rose to leave, but before they'd taken a step away from the booth, Hank Bishop approached them.

"Evening, ladies," he said in that deep, rich, Southern baritone that always created fluttering butterflies in Susan's stomach.

"Hello, Sheriff," Donna said. "Enjoy your meal?"

"Yeah, sure. It was great." Turning to Susan, he slipped his hand beneath her elbow and leaned slightly toward her. "Did you drive or did Donna?"

"Donna did. Why do you ask?"

"I was wondering…well, would you mind if I take you

home? I'd kind of like to see those sonogram pictures and—''

''Oh, sure.'' Susan widened her eyes when she looked over at Donna. ''Do you mind if Hank takes me home?''

''No, not at all. You two go right ahead,'' Donna said.

Conversation on the drive to Susan's house was limited. They briefly discussed the cold, snowy weather. Then he told her that Carl Bates's trial had been set to begin in early March. Finally the man who had killed Lowell was behind bars and would soon be judged by twelve of his peers. Hank had brought Lowell's killer to justice, just as he'd said he would. And once she delivered the baby and they were both well, Hank would have accomplished his mission here in Crooked Oak. He would have nothing to hold him here. Nothing except a woman who loved him—and a son.

''Would you like some coffee or—''

''Nothing to drink, thanks,'' he said.

Susan turned on the lights in the den, laid her handbag down on the sofa, then started to take off her coat. Suddenly, Hank was behind her, his hands on her shoulders. She tensed at his touch. He eased the coat off her and hung it in the hall closet. Susan sat down, opened her purse and removed the photographs of the sonogram. When Hank walked back into the den after hanging up their coats, she held the pictures up to him.

''Here are the first pictures of our son,'' she said.

Hank froze, staring at the pictures in Susan's outstretched hand. ''Our son? The baby's a boy?''

''Take a look and see for yourself. The pictures are kind of grainy and you might not be able to make much out of them, but if you look closely, you can see his head and the shape of his body and the part that identifies him as male.''

Hank took the pictures from her and sat down beside her

on the sofa. He stared at the snapshots, one by one, then repeated the process.

Susan held her breath while he studied the sonogram pictures. What was he thinking? What was he feeling? Were these blurry little photographs affecting him as profoundly as the sight of their child had affected her during the sonogram procedure?

"I wish Lowell were here to see these," Hank said as he handed the pictures back to Susan. "He'd be tickled to death that the baby's a boy. Lowell would have made a great father. He'd have taken the boy hunting and fishing and coached his Little League team. And he'd have set a good example for him."

"Lowell would have been a really good father to my baby." Susan laid the snapshots on the coffee table. "He was a good husband to me, but... Lowell isn't my husband anymore and he'll never get the chance to be a father to this baby—" She reached out and grabbed Hank's hand, then laid it over her slightly protruding tummy, "But you could be a father to your son. You could be a—"

He snatched his hand off her belly, then grabbed her by the shoulders, his fierce gaze halting her midsentence. "I can't be the kind of father Lowell would have been. Don't you understand? This baby was never meant to be mine. He's supposed to be Lowell's kid, not mine. I never wanted children. I still don't—"

She was crying. Dammit, he'd made her cry. Why the hell had he invited himself over here tonight? Why hadn't he left well enough alone? He'd done a good job of avoiding her since the holidays, why had he let his curiosity about the sonogram, about the baby's sex, lure him into Susan's home?

Because you care, he thought to himself. You care about Susan and you care about the baby. Her baby.

His baby.

He ran his hands down her arms, caressing her tenderly. "Don't cry, honey. Please, don't cry."

She looked at him with misty eyes, then took his hand in hers and brought it back to her stomach, back to rest over the small, ball-shaped mound of her belly.

"He's moving," she said. "Can you feel him?"

Her stomach fluttered, as if a tiny bird were trapped inside her. Suddenly Hank felt as if someone had knocked all the wind out of him. God in heaven, that was his child moving inside her. Alive, healthy and very real.

He blew out a long, deep breath. She placed her hand over his where it rested on her stomach. "It's an incredible feeling."

"Ah, Susan… This is wrong. I shouldn't be here." I shouldn't be enjoying this, his thoughts continued. I shouldn't be so damned interested. I don't want kids. *Are you sure?* an inner voice asked him.

"You can reject this child," Susan said. "But it doesn't change the fact that he's yours."

"Honey, I don't want—"

She covered his lips with her fingers. "I've missed you so much. I can't forget about the night we made love. It was the most wonderful night of my life." Scooting closer, she draped her arms around his neck and whispered against his lips, "But once wasn't enough for me. Was once enough for you?"

Run. Run like hell. She's weaving her silky, feminine web around you and if you don't leave now, you'll regret it.

She brushed her lips across his. He sucked in his breath. She lowered her hands and undid the top two buttons on his shirt, all the while smiling seductively at him. He didn't move. He sat there, ramrod straight, afraid to even breathe. She completely unbuttoned his shirt, spread it apart and laid her hands on his chest. Her small hands were hot. She flicked first one tiny nipple and then the other. Her short, oval nails repeated the process until he couldn't restrain the moan deep in his throat.

She kissed his neck, then made tantalizing little nips from his collarbone to his washboard-lean belly. She undid his belt, unbuttoned his slacks and lowered the zipper. When she reached inside to circle him through the thin barrier of his briefs, he grabbed her hand. The corners of her mouth curved upward into a confident smile.

She's got you, ole son, and she knows it. She's playing you like a fiddle. You've got two choices—stop her or join her.

"Are you sure you want to do this?" he asked.

"I've never been more sure of anything in my life," she said.

The minute he released his hold on her hand, she fondled him and was rewarded with a deep, growling moan. But before she could proceed any further, Hank grabbed her and kissed her, like a thirsty man drinking his fill of life-sustaining water. He ravaged her mouth as he lowered her onto the sofa. While he kissed her, he worked the zipper down on her loose-fitting velour shirt, then removed it and tossed it aside. Once he disposed of her bra, he concentrated on her breasts—round and full and larger than they'd been the last time he'd seen them. He braced himself above her, careful not to press his weight on her stomach, ever mindful that his child was nestled snugly inside.

They tore at each other's clothes until they were both naked. Their mouths continued to mate in a frenzy of need. Hank lifted her up and into his lap, then brought her down over his shaft. She cried out from pleasure as he filled her. He cupped her hips in his hands and worked her back and forth, letting the friction build and build, until they were both breathless. Then he slowed the pace, knowing if he didn't, he would be finished before she had a chance to fully enjoy the ride.

He felt her body clutching him, surrounding him, urging him into movement. He leaned her backward and took one tight nipple into his mouth. She moaned. He tormented her breasts until she begged him to end the sweet torture. He slipped his hand between their bodies and rubbed her intimately. She gasped. He lifted her higher onto his shaft and began again the rhythmic strokes that carried them deeper and deeper into pure sensation. As the pressure built, as they descended so deep that neither thought they'd ever return, they clung to each other. Sweat coated their hot, flushed bodies. The pace intensified. Harder. Faster. Harder. Faster. And suddenly their mutual climaxes shot through them like fire, burning them with white-hot pleasure.

The aftershocks of fulfillment rippled through their bodies as Hank eased Susan down onto the sofa and settled his big body alongside her slender frame. He held her, stroking her damp flesh, kissing her tenderly, whispering sweet nothings in her ear.

They lay there for several minutes, quiet and totally sated, and then the chill of the room hit them. Hank reached up, dragged the afghan off the back of the couch and covered them. They dozed off to sleep for over an hour.

Hank woke slowly, totally aware of the warm, naked body lying in his arms. Susan. His sex pulsed. He wanted her again!

He kissed her awake. She opened her eyes and smiled at him.

"I can go now or I can stay awhile longer," he said. "It's your decision, honey."

As she snuggled against him, she reached down and circled his shaft. "Stay."

And he did. He stayed for another two hours, upstairs in Aunt Alice's big antique bed. They made love slowly, tenderly, exploring the uniqueness of each other's bodies, learning the special places to touch.

The digital alarm clock on her nightstand read one-fifteen when Hank got up and went downstairs to retrieve his clothes. Susan slipped on a robe and followed him. She watched him dress, then walked over and put her arms around him.

"Do you have to leave?" she asked.

"You know I do. People will talk if they see my Lexus here in the morning."

"So, you're just going to come and go. We aren't going to get to spend any nights together?"

"Susan…" He grasped her face in his hands. "I keep doing this to you, don't I? I keep using you and then running away."

"Are you going to run away again?" she asked.

"Yeah, honey, I'm afraid I am. And this time, it has to be for good."

"But I thought…I had hoped that we—"

He kissed her. Quick. Hard. Then he released his hold on her. "I love making love to you. And if we weren't living in this one-horse town, with morals from the nineteenth century, and if you weren't pregnant, we might have us a wild and wooly affair. But folks around here wouldn't understand Lowell's widow and his best friend carrying on the way we've been doing. And how would you ever explain our affair to your son?"

"I suppose I could tell our son that I was in love with his father and I didn't feel any shame in having made love with him."

"Dammit, Susan, don't do this! Don't pretend that you and I and the baby have a future together."

"Can you really walk away from me—from us—without any regrets?"

"Oh, I've got regrets, honey. A ton of them. I wish I were the man you want me to be. I wish I could love you and love the baby and want to settle down here in Crooked

Oak and be the kind of husband Lowell was and the kind of father he would have been. But it's not in me to be that kind of man. I'm sorry.''

He retrieved his coat from the hall closet, gave her one final farewell glance and walked out the door.

Susan watched him leave, all the while the words she wanted to shout at him stuck in her throat.

But I don't want you to be the kind of husband Lowell was. He never made me feel the way you do. I never loved him half as much as I love you. And I don't expect you to be the kind of father Lowell was. I just want you to be the best father you know how to be. I need you. Your son needs you. Please, please, don't leave us.

Nine

Carl Bates's trial lasted twelve days. Susan sat in the court-
room each day and endured not only listening to the details
of her husband's murder and his killer being defended, but
she had to withstand Hank's silent stare of disapproval.
Each quiet look spoke volumes. But who was he to censure
her actions? Maybe he was genuinely concerned about her
and about her baby. But as far as she was concerned, he
had no rights of any kind. He had made it abundantly clear
that beyond doing his duty as Lowell's best friend, his future didn't include her or her child.

Although Susan had assured them that she didn't need
them at her side, Sheila and Donna took turns coming to
court with her each day. Today they were both there, along
with Caleb. And Tallie and Peyton had driven in from
Nashville this morning to be present for the jury's verdict.
Hank stood tall and straight against the outer wall, the Marshall County deputies at his side.

Susan's heart raced when the jurors returned, one by one, solemn-faced and with gazes cast to the floor. A low murmur spread throughout the room, the sound surrounding her, bombarding her. The voices blurred and blended, but the sentiment their muted words proclaimed were her own. This would soon be over and she could rest easy knowing Lowell's murderer would pay for his crime.

The judge entered, sat, pounded his gavel and called the court to order. Susan's stomach lurched and a bout of nausea hit her full-force. She should have eaten breakfast. But she'd been so nervous that the thought of food hadn't appealed to her. *Please, Lord, don't let me be sick. Not now, of all times.*

Donna leaned over and whispered, "Are you all right? You're white as a sheet."

"Just a little sick to my stomach," Susan assured her.

When the verdict was read—Guilty!—Susan gasped audibly. Tears gathered in her eyes as she grabbed Donna's arm.

Thank you, dear Lord. Thank you.

The crowd went wild. The judge called for order. The people of Marshall County quieted until the judge downed his gavel and quickly concluded the trial. The citizens who had so dearly loved Lowell rushed toward his widow as she rose from her seat. Caleb stepped around his wife and grasped Susan's arm. Donna moved out of the way of the ensuing horde.

"Guess folks in this state will see how Marshall County deals with murderers," the mayor said as he pushed his way toward Susan.

"Bates's life is as good as over," another man said.

"Lowell can rest in peace, now," said someone else.

"We can thank Hank Bishop for bringing Bates in," came another comment from the crowd.

"Bet you feel mighty good about this, don't you, Mrs.

Redman?'' Sammy White, a reporter for the *Marshallton Chronicle* asked.

"Any comment, Mrs. Redman?" A local TV reporter thrust a microphone in Susan's face. "How did you feel when you heard the verdict?"

The noise of hundreds of voices reverberated inside Susan's head, combining with the drumming of her own racing heartbeat. Her knees felt weak. Suddenly the room spun around and around. *Oh, Lord! Oh, Lord!*

Hank saw the stricken look on her face, her expression like that of a trapped animal with nowhere to run. Forcefully, he made his way through the celebrators. The minute she swayed, he knew she was going to faint. Caleb momentarily turned away from Susan, apparently trying to persuade the people crushing in on them to move aside and give them room to exit.

Catch her, Caleb. Dammit, catch her! his mind screamed.

She was going down. Down. Down. Caleb turned, reached out and grabbed Susan, saving her from hitting the floor. The crowd separated as Hank ran toward her. They stood back and watched as he took her from his brother and swept her up into his arms. The path to the outer door cleared as Hank marched through, a limp Susan lying against his chest. He carried her outside and straight to his Lexus.

Susan regained consciousness just as Hank slipped her into the front seat. She opened her eyes and looked up at him.

"What happened?" she asked.

"You fainted, honey." He caressed her cheek tenderly. "And no wonder. Half the population of Marshall County had you surrounded and those damn reporters were shooting questions at you."

"I—I didn't eat any breakfast this morning and I was feeling nauseated and—"

"I think I should run you over to Dr. Farr's and let him check you out."

"No. Really, Hank. I'm all right. Could you just get someone to take me home?"

"I'll take you."

"But shouldn't you—"

"They can handle things without me."

He slammed the door, rounded the hood and got in on the driver's side. He wanted to say that he'd cautioned her not to spend every day in court, listening to all the details, putting herself through the agony of reliving Lowell's death all over again. But would she listen to him? No, of course not. Not Susan. Stubborn little mule!

"Do you want me to stop and get you something to eat or drink?" he asked as he drove away from the courthouse.

"Nothing to eat. Not yet. But a ginger ale might settle my stomach."

"Sit tight, honey, I'll take care of you."

Within twenty minutes, he pulled his Lexus into Susan's driveway. She held the nearly empty ginger ale bottle in her hand. Neither of them had said much on the trip from the courthouse to Susan's home. He wasn't sure why she was so quiet, but he knew why he'd kept his mouth shut. If he said what he was thinking, he'd make her angry. And the last thing he wanted to do right now was upset Susan any more than she was already.

Mrs. Brown and Mrs. Dobson had both been in court today. Hank breathed a sigh of relief that neither neighbor was nearby, lurking in the bushes or on their front porches, waiting to pounce on him and Susan with a hundred and one questions.

He opened the passenger side door for her and when she started to get out, he lifted her up into his arms.

"I can walk," she told him.

"Just shut up, will you?"

Dammit, didn't she have any idea how he felt? How he'd felt every day of the trial, seeing her in court, watching the pain in her eyes, knowing the extent of her mourning. He had tried to tell her the first day, but she wouldn't listen. He had worried about her and about the baby, afraid the mental and emotional stress of the trial would hurt them. And he'd been right.

But she had as good as told him that what she did was none of his business. All or nothing. That's what Susan wanted—what she expected. But he couldn't give her everything—not marriage, not the forever-after kind of life she'd had with Lowell. But even Lowell couldn't give her the forever-after happiness she deserved. Didn't she realize that nothing was forever—not affairs or marriages and not even love?

When he reached the front porch, he halted. "Give me your key, so I can unlock the door."

"If you'd just put me down, I could unlock the door myself." She squirmed in his arms.

"Be still." He spoke softly but firmly. If she didn't stop arguing, he wasn't going to be responsible for his actions. "Give me the damn key."

Susan clutched her purse to her chest. Reluctantly, she opened the leather bag, rummaged around inside and withdrew her key chain. "Here, take it!"

He unlocked and opened the door, carried her into the foyer and closed the door behind them. The mutts met them, yapping and sniffing in greeting. The two felines perched on the landing upstairs and stared down at them. Susan kept her arm securely around Hank's neck as he carried her down the hall and into the den. He deposited her on the big, comfortable sofa that was draped with a floral chintz slipcover. When he tried to remove her jacket, she slapped his hands away, took off the jacket and handed it to him. Fred and Ricky lay on the rug in front of the sofa.

"What next?" she asked. "I'm home safe and sound. There's no reason for you to stay."

"I'm staying."

"Why?"

"I'm getting fed up with this attitude of yours," he warned her. When he noticed the astonished look on her face, he forced himself not to grin. "You're staying put on that sofa. I don't want you to move. Understand?"

"No, I don't—"

"You're going to rest and relax and let me take care of you. Now, stay put. I'll fix you something to eat."

"I'm not—"

"I don't care whether you're hungry or not. You need something in your stomach. How about some soup and crackers?"

"Oh, all right. Soup and crackers will be fine."

"Why don't you lie down, see if you can nap. I'll bet you haven't been sleeping well lately, have you?"

"No, I haven't."

He placed two square pillows at the end of the sofa, grasped her shoulders and eased her down, then removed her shoes and covered her, up to her waist, with the afghan he'd taken off the back of the sofa.

"Close your eyes," he said.

She did as he instructed, succumbing to the pleasure of having Hank take care of her. Enjoy it while it lasts, she told herself. All this fuss he's making over you doesn't mean a thing. He's doing his duty—taking care of Lowell's widow.

She heard the closet door open and close. He'd hung up

her jacket. Then the sweetly delicious strands of Shumann's "Dreaming" filled the room with the tender, emotional piano music. He'd turned on the CD player. She sighed. She had left one of her Classical Treasures CD's on the player. Debussy and Chopin and Beethoven would follow Shumann. Romantic music, created from the depths of the composers' souls.

Within minutes her entire body relaxed into the sofa cushions. The headache that had plagued her all day began to ease. She heard the echoes of cupboard doors opening and closing and the clatter of pots and pans. Hank Bishop was loose in her kitchen. Heaven forbid! But how much harm could he do opening a can of soup?

Surrounding her with tender, loving care had been second nature to Lowell. He had been the dearest, kindest man in the world. And often she had felt unworthy of him. And guilty that she didn't love him more. But she had never lied to him about how she felt, never pretended that theirs was a passionate love match. But Lowell hadn't seemed to care. He had loved her, been devoted to her and treated her like a queen. The love and respect and compatibility they shared had made up for any lack of passion in their marriage.

My poor, darling Lowell. If only you were here. If only you hadn't died and left me. Tears gathered in the corners of her eyes and trickled down into her hair and over the tips of her ears. She lay there, quietly, sobbing softly so that Hank couldn't hear her.

She had almost dozed off when Hank came back into the den. She felt his presence, then opened her eyes and stared up at him. He stood there holding a large tray and watching her intently.

"Are you feeling any better?" he asked.

"Much, thank you."

"Do you want to eat now? I've got vegetable soup

here—'' he nodded to the large bowl on the tray ''—a grilled cheese sandwich and a glass of milk.''

As if on cue, her stomach rumbled. Smiling, she eased herself up into a sitting position and slid her legs off the side of the sofa. ''Actually, I am hungry.''

He placed the tray in her lap, then sat beside her. ''Try not to think about the trial anymore. Carl Bates is going to prison for the rest of his life. My guess is that Judge Ware will give him life without parole. So, it's all over, honey. Time to let it go and move on with your life.''

''Carl Bates spending the rest of his life in prison won't bring Lowell back, but it will keep him from ever harming anyone else. And as far as it being all over...well, it was all over the night Lowell died. Nothing will ever be the same without him.''

''Yeah, I know.'' Hank wanted to take her in his arms and comfort her, but he knew that if he touched her, comforting wasn't all he'd do. ''Come on. Eat up, while it's hot.''

The canned vegetable soup was delicious and even the slightly burned grilled cheese sandwich tasted good. She'd gone too long without food. She wouldn't do that again.

When she finished off the last drop of her milk, Hank took the tray and returned to the kitchen. She got to her feet and followed him. He stood at the sink, washing the dirty dishes.

''You could've just left those,'' she told him. ''Or put them in the dishwasher.''

''Not enough to fool with the dishwasher,'' he said. ''What are you doing in here, anyway? You're supposed to be resting.''

''I'm all right, now.'' She stood just inside the doorway, waiting for him to turn around and look at her. ''Hank?''

''Yeah.'' He still had his back to her.

''I've missed you.''

His big, broad shoulders tensed. He placed the bowl and the glass on the drainboard and then turned around slowly.

"I've missed you, too, honey."

"Don't you think you could stop by every once in a while? We could sit and talk and... Don't you think we could handle our...our attraction to each other, now that I'm not so attractive." The corners of her mouth lifted in a weak, halfhearted smile.

"What do you mean, now that you aren't attractive?"

"Well, look at me." She ran her hands over her protruding tummy. "I'm six and half months' pregnant and I'm—"

"Beautiful." He crossed the room hurriedly, halting directly in front of her.

She took in a deep breath when she saw the look of desire in his eyes. "You think I'm beautiful?"

He knew that if he touched her, he'd be lost. But, God help him, he wanted to touch her more than anything. "I think you're the most beautiful thing I've ever seen. Tummy and all." He grinned.

The bottom dropped out of her stomach. Why did he have to go and say something so darn wonderful? "You won't come back, after today, will you?"

"No."

"It's so unfair." She reached out to touch him, but he backed away from her. "Lowell should be alive and I should be in love with him. And this—" she laid her hand over her belly "—should be his baby."

"You're right on all counts. Lowell deserved a better deal than he got."

"He knew I wasn't in love with him." She focused on Hank's black eyes, wishing she could see past the surface, into his soul. "But he never knew how I felt about you. And the strange thing is, I think that if I'd told him, he would have understood."

"He was crazy about you." Hank closed his eyes to shut out the sight of her. "I remember when he came to see me to ask me to be the sperm donor for your artificial insemination. He kept saying how much he wanted you to have a baby, that you were the kind of woman who'd never be complete without a child. That man would have walked over burning hot coals for you."

"Yes, I know." Susan closed the distance between them, reached up and cupped Hank's face with her hands. "You and I were the two most important people in Lowell's life. He loved us both and we loved him. He would want to see us happy. Don't you know that if he could, he'd tell you that you don't have to feel guilty for caring about me?" She reached down, grasped Hank's hand and held it over her belly. "He'd want you to love this child and be a father to him."

Hank pulled her into his arms, hugging her close, stroking her hair, whispering her name repeatedly. She melted against him, as if the heat of his body had seeped into her and bonded them together. He kissed her forehead and her temples and then her cheeks.

Glorying in his touch, she lifted her face and offered him her lips. "Don't leave. Stay with me tonight. I need you so, Hank."

He took her mouth in a hot, hungry kiss that conveyed his desire. She clung to him as he wrapped her securely in his powerful embrace. When he deepened the kiss, he eased her up against the wall.

Suddenly they heard a loud rapping at the back door. Hank broke the kiss, lifted and turned his head just enough to see through the glass section of the kitchen door. God Almighty! Caleb was peering into the house. Sheila was at his side.

"It's my damn family," Hank said. "I should have known that they would have to come by to check on you."

Susan was well aware of her mussed hair, flushed face and swollen lips when Caleb, Sheila, Tallie, Peyton and Donna entered the kitchen.

"Good thing we were the first to arrive," Tallie said. "Y'all might have had some difficulty explaining the situation, if it hadn't been us."

Hank shuffled uneasily. Susan's face reddened even more.

"Half the town of Crooked Oak is on the way," Caleb said. "Folks want to celebrate this victory with Lowell's widow. You can expect dozens of people to stop by anytime now."

"They're bringing food and have plans for a party," Sheila said.

"Oh." Susan looked at Hank. "I had no idea."

The back door swung open. Mrs. Brown and Mrs. Dobson breezed in as if they weren't intruding. Each carried a covered dish.

"I see y'all have started without us," Mrs. Brown said. "Now, Susan, dear, you just go on and greet your guests at the front door. Teenie and I will take care of all the food and arrange everything on the dining table."

"Yes, thank you." Susan continued staring at Hank, wishing he would say something, react in some way.

Tallie laced her arm though Susan's and led her out of the kitchen. By the time they entered the den, the doorbell rang.

"Do you want me to get it?" Sheila asked.

"Yes, would you, please?" Susan replied.

Within fifteen minutes her house was filled to capacity with the same group of people who had, only five months ago, shared her grief over Lowell's death. Now they were sharing the relief that Lowell's killer had been tried and convicted.

Hank stayed for about an hour, mingling and mixing with

the citizenry. Then he made his way over to her. She knew before he spoke that he was leaving.

"I'm heading out," he said. "I need to stop back by the office for a while." He didn't touch her, didn't even take her hand. But she knew he wanted to touch her, knew by the way he was looking at her that he'd like nothing better than to take her upstairs and make love to her. "I'll call you in the morning."

"Yes, please call."

"If you need me—"

She lowered her voice to a whisper. "You aren't coming back, are you? Not tonight or any other night."

He didn't respond. He didn't have to—she knew the answer. Once again Hank was walking out on her. Running scared. And she didn't know what she could say or do that would change his mind—now or ever. She couldn't make him love her. Couldn't force him to put aside his fears and uncertainties. Time was running out for Hank and her.

Losing Lowell had been difficult, but she had survived. But if she lost Hank…

Susan excused herself to go to the bathroom. She sat on the cushioned stool and laid her head on the vanity table. Donna eased opened the door, came inside and walked over to Susan.

"Are you all right?" Donna asked.

Susan lifted her head and stared up at her friend. "No, I'm not all right. And if I lose Hank, I don't think I'll ever be all right again."

Ten

"**I** have to sit down," Donna said. "My feet are killing me."

Susan glanced over at her friend, who at seven and half months' pregnant was round as a barrel. "Why don't you go to my office and rest for a while? You've done more than enough this morning to help me. I think Scooter and I can handle things by ourselves until Sheila gets here. The real crowds won't show up until nearly noon. Everyone loves Ella Higgins's chicken stew and Jerry Smith's barbeque, so nobody's going to miss lunch."

"Oh, I forgot to tell you that they delivered the cola machines while you were helping Mr. Murphy set up the loudspeaker." Donna lifted one foot and then the other. "I think my ankles are swollen. God, nobody ever told me that being pregnant would turn me into a water-logged cow." She glared at Susan. "Of course, not all of us get big as barns. Just look at you. You're nearly seven months' pregnant and you're still a beanpole."

"A beanpole with a watermelon attached." Susan laughed as she rubbed her belly. Standing behind Donna, she grasped her shoulders. "Go. Scoot. Get off your feet. I'll holler, if I need you."

As Donna headed straight for Susan's office, Sheila Bishop drove into the parking lot at the animal shelter. She got out, spoke to Donna and then waved at Susan.

Susan didn't know what she'd do without good friends and staunch supporters of the shelter. Without a lot of help, she'd never be able to pull off the annual fund-raiser that brought in a quarter of the revenue for the shelter. Animal lovers throughout the county pitched in to help, volunteering their time and services. The yearly event had become well-known throughout the county and surrounding areas. People seemed to love its carnival-like atmosphere. Scooter always dressed up as a clown. Ladies brought in homemade baked goods. Ella Higgins prepared her famous stew and gave all the profits to the shelter, and Jerry Smith, who owned the local barbeque restaurant, also donated his profits for the day. And every year, Mrs. Brown donated a handmade quilt, which was auctioned off to the highest bidder.

The townsfolk masqueraded as fortune tellers, magicians and belly dancers. Bill Tompkins demonstrated his sharpshooter skills with his Winchester rifle and Hoyt Dover always brought in several of his antique cars to display.

The fund-raiser was strictly small-town stuff, but it attracted the people of Marshall County and usually brought in visitors from neighboring counties. Susan suspected that the simple, old-time atmosphere of the event produced the special charm that attracted most people. These days everyone seemed immersed in nostalgia.

"Caleb and Danny will be on in about an hour," Sheila said. "They're loading up now. Danny's so excited that he and his father are going to have their own mini-baseball card show here at the April Fool's Fair."

"I'm glad you came early," Susan said. "Donna's been here since seven and she's worn herself out."

"Poor Donna. She looks like she's going to have twins, doesn't she?"

"Not twins, just one very big girl."

"Wonder how big a man that big baby girl's daddy is?"

"Has Donna ever told you any details about him?" Susan asked.

"Nothing more than she told you. His friends called him J.B., he was a rough, crude cowboy, and they did it like rabbits for a couple of days. That's about it."

Susan giggled. "Lord, that sounded awful."

"I, er, I have something to tell you," Sheila said.

"So, you had an ulterior motive for coming early. And here I thought you'd come to help."

Sheila hit Susan playfully on the arm. "I have two cakes and three pies in the trunk of my car, and I am ready, willing and able to follow your orders. But..."

"But what?"

"I may have to excuse myself if the morning sickness I've been experiencing the past few days kicks in."

"What? Morning sickness!" Susan shrieked, then grabbed Sheila and hugged her. "You're pregnant. You and Caleb are going to have another child."

"He's so happy," Sheila said. "He regrets that he missed being around when I was pregnant with Danny, so he's excited at the prospect of sharing this pregnancy with me."

"You're very lucky." Susan hugged Sheila again, then released her. "You've never loved anyone except Caleb and now he loves you just as much as you do him. All your dreams have come true."

"Oh, hon, maybe things will work out for you and Hank.

The guy's such a stubborn jackass. All the Bishop men are. Caleb didn't think of himself as husband material, either. But even though he didn't consider himself the marrying kind, he was. And so is Hank. I'd say Jake is the only one of the three who isn't fit for marriage. He was the wild one, wasn't he? I pity the poor woman who falls for him.''

"I appreciate that you've invited Hank and me out to your place for dinner twice in the past couple of weeks. Coming out to your farm at least gave me a chance to see him and talk to him in person. But I'm afraid it didn't do much good. He hasn't made a move on his own.''

"Oh, I wouldn't say that it didn't do much good,'' Sheila said. "Anybody with half a brain could tell by the way Hank looks at you that he's crazy about you. Sooner or later, he's bound to work through his fear of marriage and fatherhood.''

"Do you honestly think Hank's in love with me?''

"Yes, I do. And so does Caleb. But we don't think Hank has figured it out, yet. He's never been in love before, so he really has no idea that what he's experiencing is love.''

Susan smiled, a feeling of hope spreading through her— the first real hope she'd had since the last time Hank had walked out on her.

"I wonder if he'll show up here today.''

"Sure he will,'' Sheila said. "He's the sheriff. It would look kind of odd if he didn't put in an appearance.''

Hank nodded and spoke to several people as he made his way through the crowd at the annual April Fool's Day fund-raiser. He'd heard folks talking about the event—even his deputies couldn't say enough about the shindig that Susan Williams Redman put on every year to raise extra, much needed money for her animal shelter. And that's how people thought of the shelter—not as Crooked Oak's shelter, but as Susan's. She'd been the shelter's manager for ten years, ever since old Mr. Mayhew had retired from the position he'd held most of his life. During her lifetime, Alice Williams had been the shelters most generous benefactress and had even bequeathed the shelter a tidy sum. The Williams women had a real affinity with animals. A lot of people said that Miss Alice and Susan treated animals better than some folks treated their kids. A testament to their love for God's creatures and a sad statement about those who were blessed with children they didn't deserve.

Hank's own parents had been among those unworthy. Irresponsible. Self-centered. Unsuitable for the awesome task of raising children. And the dumb fools had reproduced four damn times. His mama had spit the four of them out in rapid succession and then she'd gone and gotten herself killed. He'd been just a boy when it happened and so had Jake, who had refused to ever discuss their parents with him. But Caleb had been a toddler and Tallie just a baby.

God! Claude Bishop had been a hard, cold man, but he'd taken in his wayward son's four brats. He'd fed them and clothed them and done his best. Sometimes, Hank wondered what would have happened to them without that proud, stubborn old man.

He didn't think much about the past anymore. Thinking about what couldn't be changed was a waste of time. But lately his thoughts had wandered backward in time—to his own childhood. He supposed it was happening because of Susan's baby. Even though he'd never wanted to be a father, the fact remained that Susan was going to give birth to his son in less than three months. A boy who needed a father. And despite all his fears and uncertainties, there was something deep inside him that wanted to be a father to his son.

The afternoon sun hung low in the bright blue sky. Hank checked his watch. Four forty-five. The fund-raiser ended at dusk and even on a sunny day like today, night would fall soon. He had deliberately waited until day's end to put in an appearance at the big event. He had no choice but to come, but he didn't have to spend half a day mooning around, lusting after Susan. And God help him, he did lust after her.

Hank passed the fortune-teller's tent and did a double take when he realized the colorfully costumed gypsy was none other than Mrs. Dobson, Susan's neighbor. The portly, silver-haired woman waved at him. He nodded and smiled at her.

"Come get your fortune told, Sheriff," she called to him. "It's just two dollars and it's for a good cause."

Reluctantly, Hank walked over to the open tent, pulled out his wallet and handed Mrs. Dobson the money. "Keep it and give somebody else a free reading." He glanced meaningfully at her crystal ball.

"How about you, Susan? Want to have your fortune told, free of charge, courtesy of Sheriff Bishop?"

Hank snapped his head around and glanced over his shoulder. There stood Susan a few feet behind him. She wore jeans and a billowing, red maternity top. She'd pulled her long brown hair up into a ponytail and wispy curls framed her face. His body stirred to life. Damn, every time he looked at her, he wanted her.

"A free reading?" Susan walked over to the tent. "How could I pass up such a good offer?" She smiled at Hank. "Hi, how are you? I was beginning to wonder if you were going to make it by today."

"Yeah, well, I made it. How's it been going? Looks like there's still a pretty big crowd."

Susan laced her arm through his and pulled him along with her inside the tent. "Come on, Hank. Stay with me until Mrs. Dob—that is, Madame Yolanda, tells my fortune."

"Sit down, my dear, and I will tell you the secrets of your future." Mrs. Dobson spoke with what was undoubtedly her idea of a foreign accent.

Susan sat and held out her hand. Mrs. Dobson lifted her hand, ran her finger over the tiny lines in Susan's palm and smiled. "I see great happiness ahead for you. A beautiful, healthy baby boy."

Susan glanced at Hank and smiled. He shrugged as if to say, "The whole world knows you're expecting a boy."

"And I see a new love for you. A love to last a lifetime. A fine, good man who will take care of you and your son." Mrs. Dobson stared pointedly at Hank.

Susan blushed. Did everyone know that she was in love with Hank Bishop? Did she give herself away every time she looked at him?

"And just when will this new love come into my life?" Susan asked. "And how will I recognize him?"

"He has already come into your life, my dear girl. And your heart will recognize him."

Susan smiled warmly. Apparently Mrs. Dobson had guessed that there was more between her and Hank than friendship, or maybe the old woman was just a romantic who was playing matchmaker.

As Mrs. Dobson gazed into the crystal ball, she swirled her hands in a grand gesture, then spoke in a low voice. "I see more children in your future. Another boy and then a little girl. A girl with black hair and eyes, like her father."

Hank shifted uncomfortably. Mrs. Dobson had zeroed in on him as a future mate for Susan. Was the old woman really psychic or was it wishful thinking on her part, hoping he'd marry and take care of Lowell's widow?

"Thank you," Susan said. "I like my fortune very much."

Mrs. Dobson clasped Susan's hands. "Be happy, sweet child. That's what Lowell would have wanted."

Susan hugged Mrs. Dobson, then stood and laced her arm through Hank's again. "Let me show you around."

"All right."

"Have you eaten?" she asked.

"Not yet."

"Well, all the chicken stew is gone, but why don't we get us some barbeque and go over to my office and eat supper together?"

"Susan, I don't think that's a good idea," he said. "I mean… Well, I hope you didn't take Mrs. Dobson's fortune-telling to heart."

Susan paused, lifted her gaze to his and smiled. "Hank Bishop, you really are scared of me, aren't you?"

"Scared of you? I don't know what you're talking about."

"All right, if you're not scared to be alone with me, then let's go get that barbeque and have supper together."

She had issued a challenge and he knew it. If he refused, he would prove her right. If he agreed, he ran the risk of winding up making love to her again.

"Let's get some barbeque," he said.

Susan wiped her mouth with the paper napkin, then tossed it on top of her plate, which was scattered with crumbs from her sandwich. She moaned contentedly. "Jerry Smith makes the best barbeque in the State of Tennessee."

"I have to agree," Hank said, then downed the last drops of his root beer. He had accepted Susan's challenge— they'd spent the last twenty minutes alone together in her office. They'd eaten dinner together and talked about unimportant, mundane matters like the weather and a recent TV movie they'd both watched and this morning's regional newspaper headlines about a Marshall County resident winning a Caribbean vacation.

Susan shifted her hips, gaining a more comfortable position on the sofa. She looked at Hank, who sat in her swivel chair, his feet propped up on her desk. Why did he have to look so good? Big and lean and handsome. Every time she saw him, she remembered what it had been like to lie in his arms, to have his lips and hands caressing her, to know the pleasure of his lovemaking. She wondered if he could see the longing in her eyes the way she saw it in his.

"Did Caleb tell you the news about Sheila and him?" Susan asked.

"I haven't talked to Caleb in a few days," Hank said. "What's the news?"

"Sheila's pregnant."

Hank nodded. The expression on his face showed his surprise. "Looks like Caleb is fitting right into the domestic life. I'm glad things have worked out for Sheila and him. I have to admit that I had my doubts when he first told me that they were going to get married."

"Why did you have doubts?" Susan asked. "They were in love and wanted to spend the rest of their lives together."

"Yeah, I know. It's just that Caleb had been a playboy for quite a few years. I wasn't sure he was really ready to settle down and be a family man."

"He's a wonderful husband and a really good father to Danny."

"Look, Susan, I..." Hank eased his feet off the desk. "I've been thinking about the baby. About your child."

"What about my baby?" Her heart stopped beating for one tiny millimeter of a second.

"I've been thinking about how a boy needs a father and that since...well, technically, I am his father..."

"Yes, *technically,* you are," she agreed.

"I don't know what kind of father I'd be." He scooted

back the chair and stood. "I didn't have much of an example. My grandfather was a hardworking, honest man, but he was too hard and cold to be a real father to us. And you know what a failure my old man was."

"Just because your father and grandfather weren't the best fathers in the world doesn't mean that you can't be a good father."

"I don't want to become a part of this kid's life and then let him down, disappoint him." Hank came around the desk and moved toward Susan.

She waited, her heart beating ninety to nothing, her mind whirling with the possibilities that Hank's new attitude presented. "Do you want to be a father to this baby?"

When he sat beside her, she reached out, took his hand and placed it over her tummy. Their son chose that precise moment to make his presence known.

"Wow! What a kick! This kid will probably play football for U.T." Hank pressed his hand gently over the small foot that punched at him through Susan's belly. "That doesn't hurt you, does it, his kicking like that?"

"No, not really, but sometimes your son balls up in one spot and the pressure can become uncomfortable. And I usually can't get him to budge. Looks like he's as stubborn as you are."

Hank didn't know how to deal with what he was feeling—with the knowledge that this tiny life inside Susan was his child and that he really did want to be a father to this baby. He had fought long and hard against his paternal feelings for his son, but he'd lost the fight.

"I want to be more than a godfather to my son," Hank told her.

She slipped her arms around his neck and gazed adoringly into his eyes. "You'll be a wonderful father. Just wait and see."

All he could see at that precise moment was Susan—

soft, warm, beautiful, and so very close. He pulled her into his arms. God, how he loved the feel of her. He loved the way she looked, the way she moved, the way she talked and even the way she smelled. Always sweet and fresh, like springtime flowers.

He kissed her with a tender passion, knowing that he was going to make love to her again. It was this way between them every time they touched. An uncontrollable desire consumed them.

The door to Susan's office flew open. "Susan, my dear, I've just counted the money and we—" Mrs. Brown's feet skidded on the wooden floor as she came to an abrupt halt. "Oh, my, my. Please, excuse me. I didn't realize... I'm so sorry." She turned and scurried out of the office, departing so hurriedly that she left the door wide open.

Hank muttered a sharp, succinct vulgarity. Susan bit down on her bottom lip. The two stared at each other and then suddenly burst into laughter.

"We shouldn't be laughing, honey. Mrs. Brown is probably running around out there telling everyone she knows that she caught us kissing."

"I don't care," Susan said. "I don't care if the whole world knows we were kissing."

"If you don't care, neither do I. We'll find a way to deal with the town's reaction to our relationship."

"Do we have a relationship?" Susan asked.

"Yes, I think we do," he told her. "If I spend the night with you tonight, then everyone will know that there's more going on between us than friendship."

"Are you going to spend the night with me tonight?"

"If you'll let me, I am."

Pleasure as warm as April sunshine spread throughout Susan's body and seeped into her heart. Hank wasn't going to desert her, wasn't going to leave her alone to raise their child. He wanted to be a father. She knew, in her heart of hearts, that it was only a matter of time until he proposed.

She threw her arms around his neck, closed her eyes and said a silent prayer of thanks. Everything is going to be all right, now, she assured herself. Hank and I and our baby are going to be a family.

Susan felt strangely awkward allowing Hank to see her naked now that she was nearly seven months' pregnant. She hadn't gained a lot of weight and wasn't retaining water the way Donna was, but her stomach was quite large and so were her breasts. How could Hank possibly find her attractive in her present condition?

She grabbed his hands when he tried to unbutton her maternity top. "I don't look the way I did the last time. I've gotten pretty big and—"

He kissed her, then cupped her face with his hands. "You're the best-looking pregnant lady I've ever seen. And if you think I don't find you attractive, then you'd better think again."

"You really find me attractive? Now. Looking like this?"

"Yes, I do. And if you'll give me a chance, I'll prove it to you."

She nodded meekly. "We'll have to be inventive since I'm sure my stomach will get in the way."

"Oh, Susie Q, I'm going to show you inventive."

Hank's wide grin set off rockets inside her—rockets that soared through her bloodstream and set her on fire.

He did a slow, sexy striptease in front of her. Then when he stood boldly naked in front of her, she made no protest as he unbuttoned her top, removed it and then unhooked her bra. He lifted her large breasts into his hands.

"Are they tender?" he asked.

"Yes. Very tender."

"Then I'll be extra careful with them."

He eased her down on the bed, slipped her maternity jeans over her hips and then removed her shoes and socks before taking off the jeans and panties. She lay before him naked and very pregnant. Pregnant with his baby. He smoothed his hand slowly from her neck, over her breasts and across her protruding belly, finally covering her mound with his palm.

"You're a mighty sexy mother-to-be," he said, his voice slightly slurred.

"And you're a sexy father-to-be," she replied breathlessly.

He explored the intimate delicacies of her body, first with his fingers and then with his mouth. Sighing her surrender as her body relaxed, she spread her legs fully and gave him dominion over her. Using his tongue, he brought her to the edge, but before he allowed her to plunge into complete fulfillment, he withdrew and began again the slow, worshipful caresses to her legs and arms. She whimpered as need built higher and higher within her. His lips covered every inch of her back and buttocks, then he turned her over with great gentleness and gave her breasts his full attention, being cautious not to be too rough.

"Please, Hank. I can't…it's too much."

"Soon. Very soon," he promised.

With his fingertips tenderly rubbing her nipples and his tongue lovingly tormenting her femininity, Hank brought Susan to the edge once more. And this time when she began to drop over into the abyss of pure sensation, he gave her the final push. She writhed and cried out, but he continued until she was mindless with pleasure.

When the fading ripples of her climax echoed through her body, Hank eased out of bed, maneuvered her to the side of the mattress and lifted her legs to his shoulders. He entered her slowly, ever mindful of her delicate condition.

She undulated her hips, inviting him to take her completely. He sank into her depths, filling her, expanding her. Susan moaned, loving the feel of him inside her.

With each thrust, his control slipped more and more, until with one final lunge he jetted his release into the welcoming warmth of her body. And as his climax hit him, Susan trembled when fulfillment claimed her a second time.

Hank eased her back into the bed, then crawled in beside her and took her into his arms. He kissed her, his lips hot and moist and infinitely tender.

When he pulled her close, she snuggled against him. "Don't leave," she whispered. "Not yet."

"I'm not going to leave," he said. "I'm going to stay all night."

"You are?" she said sleepily.

"Yes, I am. Tonight and tomorrow night and—"

After placing one finger over his lips, she lifted her head and gazed into his dark eyes. "I love you."

He kissed her on the nose. "You're the sweetest thing on earth. And I'm going to try to be what you want me to be. For you and the baby."

Susan smiled, then yawned. "You're already what I want you to be. You don't have to change. I love you just the way you are."

"Go to sleep, honey. We'll talk about this in the morning."

"All right." She sighed, yawned again and closed her eyes.

Hank lay awake for a long time, holding her, watching the moonlight shimmering across her face. He knew he had to do the right thing by Susan and the child. He had to set aside his reservations about marriage and fatherhood and accept his responsibilities. In the morning, he'd tell Susan what he had decided. She didn't have to worry about the future. He was going to take care of everything.

* * *

The ringing telephone woke Susan from a wonderful dream—a dream where she and Hank were happily married. Reaching for the phone on the nightstand, she accidently knocked over the alarm clock. She picked up the receiver, said hello and glanced over to the other side of the bed. Empty. Hank was gone. Tired from a full day at the fund-raiser and sedated on sexual fulfillment, she had slept soundly, not even aware that Hank had gotten out of bed.

"Susan? Susan, are you there?" Sheila asked.

"Huh? What? Oh, sorry, yes, I'm here."

"Is Hank still there with you?"

"What? How did you know that—"

"News travels fast," Sheila said. "Is Hank still there?"

"I don't know. He may be downstairs."

"I thought y'all should know that Mrs. Brown has spread the word that you and Hank were kissing."

"Oh, dear, I was afraid of that."

"Well, Mrs. Brown is simply delighted. She's certain a wedding isn't far off. She thinks you and Hank are a perfect match. But I'm afraid not everyone agrees."

Susan scooted to the edge of the bed, slipped her feet into her house slippers and stood. "How could word have traveled that fast? Mrs. Brown walked in on Hank kissing me late yesterday."

"Oh, that's not the worst of it." Sheila sighed heavily.

"What do you mean?"

"It seems Hank's Lexus has been spotted at your house and now everyone knows that he stayed the night with you. This fact, coupled with Mrs. Brown's tale about the passionate kiss she witnessed, has the whole town buzzing. I've had four phone calls already this morning and it's only eight o'clock."

"Damn! Why can't people just mind their own business?"

"I thought I should warn you and Hank. Let y'all know what's happening, so you can be prepared for the worst."

The bedroom door swung open. Hank walked in carrying two ceramic mugs. "Who's on the phone?" he asked as he approached Susan.

She placed her hand over the mouthpiece and replied, "It's Sheila. She's the bearer of town gossip. It seems Mrs. Brown has told the world at large about seeing us kissing. And someone spotted your Lexus parked here overnight."

Hank handed Susan the cup of hot cocoa, then took the phone from her. "Sheila, it's Hank."

"Look, you and Susan should know that the town is forming two sides—two opposing opinions on your and Susan's relationship. Some are delighted that you two are a pair. Others are appalled that y'all are carrying on so soon after Lowell's death."

"Well, Sheila, Susan and I don't care what this town thinks. But you can tell anyone else who calls you that you know for a fact that Susan and I are getting married, just as soon as possible."

"What!" Sheila shouted.

"W-what did you say?" Mumbling, Susan stared wide-eyed at Hank.

"Susan will call you later," Hank told Sheila, then hung up the receiver.

"Hank?" Susan set her mug down on the nightstand. "What do you mean, we're getting married as soon as possible?"

Hank placed his mug beside Susan's, then gently clasped her shoulders. "I've given it a lot of thought, honey. And it's the only sensible thing to do. You're pregnant with my child and our son needs a father. I'll admit that I'm scared at the very idea of trying to be a good father and a good husband, but I can't think of any other solution. Lowell's death left you and your baby alone. It's my duty to step in and take Lowell's place.

"And it's not like you and I aren't good together. A lot of couples don't even have that going for them. Of course, it would mean your moving to Alexandria with me when I go back to work for the Bureau. We'll buy a house, of course. I don't expect you and the baby to live in my apartment."

Susan stared at him as she listened to what he was saying. The words that rang out loud and clear were *sensible* and *solution* and *duty*. He hadn't mentioned love. Hank was offering her what she'd dreamed of—marriage to him. But in her dream Hank had loved her.

"If we start making plans today, we should be able to get married within a week," he said. "I know, under the circumstances, you won't expect a wedding. We'll have Judge Ware marry us in his chambers. And if you'd like, Caleb and Sheila can be our witnesses."

He made the whole arrangement sound like a business deal. Cold and unfeeling. How could she accept his offer when he had made it out of duty and not out of love?

She wanted to be Hank's wife more than she'd ever wanted anything in her life. And she wanted him to be a real father to his son. But how could she marry him if he didn't love her?

Susan pulled away from him. He stared at her quizzically.

"I want you to leave," she said in a calm, controlled voice.

He just stared at her, his eyes questioning her.

"I don't want you to marry me because you can't figure out any other solution, because you believe it's the right thing to do." Her voice rose to a higher volume. "I don't want you doing me any favors! You don't have to sacrifice your blessed bachelorhood for me and my baby!"

"Susan, honey, don't go getting all upset." He reached out for her, but she sidestepped his grasp. "I thought marriage was what you wanted. I thought you'd be happy that I'd finally come around to your way of thinking."

"Get out!" she screamed at him.

"Susan?"

"Dammit, Hank Bishop, get out of my sight right this minute!" She glowered at him, her jaw tight, her teeth clenched.

"All right. Just calm down. I'll leave and give you time to think things through." He hurried to the door, then paused. "I'm just trying to do what's best for all of us."

Susan picked up a glass figurine off the nightstand and pitched it at Hank's head. Barely missing him, the figurine hit the door frame, broke in two and crashed to the floor.

Hank exited hurriedly. Susan slumped down on the bed, balled her hands into fists and beat furiously at the pillows.

Damn him! How dare he propose to her in such a cold, calculated way? Duty. Responsibility. Doing the right thing. To hell with all his noble sentiments. She would gladly trade them all for one little word. Love.

She needed to talk to someone unbiased. Someone who could help her decide what she should do. She wanted nothing less than Hank's love, but she had more than herself to consider in this situation. She had to think of her child. Hank's son would need him every day of his young life. Did she have the right to reject Hank's offer and deny her son his father?

Susan lifted the telephone receiver, dialed the number and waited.

"Hello?" the male voice said.

"Reverend Swan, this is Susan Redman. I really need to talk to you this morning. Do you think I could come over in about an hour?"

"Yes, of course, Susan. Come on over."

After her bath, Susan dressed quickly, then went downstairs to feed the animals and let the dogs outside for a few minutes. Just as she entered the kitchen, a loud rumble of thunder shook the house. Great, she thought, just great. It was going to rain. The weather would fit her gloomy mood. When she started to open the refrigerator to retrieve a carton of milk, she noticed a note attached to the door.

"Fed the mutts and felines," she read, "and took the boys out to do their business. You and I will talk everything over this evening. I'll take you somewhere nice for dinner. Hank."

She jerked the note off the refrigerator, crumpled it in her hand and tossed it into the garbage. She said goodbye to Lucy, Ethel, Fred and Ricky, put on her coat and headed for her car. Just as she slid behind the driver's seat, the sky opened up and the rain came down in torrents.

She drove below the speed limit, taking extra precautions because the roads were slick and she could barely see the road in front her. As she rounded the corner at Fifth and Elm, she noticed the windows were steaming up. She turned on the defog system and within minutes the windows cleared. She noted that the light at the intersection was green. When she reached the center of the intersection, she saw that a car coming from her left was traveling at a high speed. The driver didn't slow down, didn't stop at the red light. Susan knew what was going to happen and realized, in that split second, she was powerless to stop it. The out-of-control vehicle struck the driver's side of Susan's car with a deadly force. The air bag exploded in her face. She screamed. And then everything went pitch-black.

Eleven

Hank mumbled brief replies to the greetings he received on his way into his office. He hoped the day was uneventful because he sure as hell didn't feel like putting up with crap from anybody.

He slammed the door behind him when he entered his office, checked the coffeemaker on the table in the corner and thanked God someone had thought to make a fresh pot for him. He poured the hot liquid into a mug, pulled out his chair and sat behind his desk.

What had he done wrong? He was sure Susan had wanted them to get married. So why, when he'd proposed to her this morning, had she gotten angry and ordered him to leave her house? He didn't understand women, especially one woman in particular.

Come on, Bishop, admit it, an inner voice taunted. *Your proposal was hardly the kind a woman dreams about all her life. No roses. No candlelight. No sweet music playing in the background. You should have waited until you could have set the stage for her. Hell, man, you haven't even bought her a ring yet.*

Okay, the first thing he needed to do was make reservations for dinner somewhere romantic. And then call up a couple of jewelers in Marshallton and get some quotes on diamond rings. And he should call the local florist and have a couple dozen roses sent— No, not roses, lilies. A huge bouquet of lilies.

Dinner reservations. Flowers. An engagement ring. And tonight, when he proposed again, she'd say yes.

He pulled the telephone directory out of the bottom desk drawer, flipped through the pages and stopped at the heading for restaurants. He read off the list and narrowed his choices down to three. Seafood, French cuisine, or an old lodge located on a lake. The listing for the lodge noted that they catered private parties for two to two hundred.

Hank smiled. A private party for two was just what he needed to woo and win his fair lady.

Just as he reached for the telephone, someone knocked on the office door. "Yeah?"

"Hank, it's Richard," the deputy said as he eased open the door.

"Yeah, Richard, what's up?" He took one look at his deputy's solemn face and knew something terrible had happened. "What's wrong?"

"We just got a call from the police department. There's been a bad wreck at the intersection of Fifth and Elm. A drunk driver, doing seventy, ran a red light and crashed into the side of a vehicle crossing on a green light."

"Damn! I'd like to put all drunk drivers in jail. How bad was it? Anyone killed?"

"The drunk's dead. He wasn't wearing a seat belt."

"And?"

"The woman driving the other vehicle has been rushed

to County General. She was unconscious and had lost a lot of blood. And the air bag didn't protect her much from the side blow to her minivan.''

"Minivan?"

"God, Hank, I'm sorry. It was Susan Redman. She was the other driver."

The world stopped suddenly. No sound. No light. No feeling. Utter and complete desolation. And then he heard the beating of his own heart. He could see Richard Holman's lips moving, but he couldn't understand anything he said. Hank's body was engulfed in icy fear. Numbness dissolved into pinpricks of pain, stabbing his whole body.

Susan had been in an accident. What if she was badly hurt? What if she lost the baby? What if she died?

Hank felt a hand on his shoulder. He turned to look at his deputy.

"Come on," Richard said. "I'll drive you over to County General."

"How—" Hank cleared his throat. "How bad is she hurt?"

Richard patted Hank on the back. "Pretty bad."

They arrived at County General's emergency room fifteen minutes later. The ER staff informed Hank that Mrs. Redman was in surgery on the second floor. He didn't wait to ask any questions, but once he and Richard were in the elevator, he turned to his deputy.

"I want you to call Caleb and Sheila," Hank said.

"Already took care of that," Richard said. "Before we left the office, I told Helen to call your brother."

"Thanks."

What the hell was taking the elevator so long to move up one damn floor? He had to get to Susan. Had to be there. Had to do something to save her. Just as he reminded himself how irrational his thoughts were, the elevator doors swung open. Hank flew out and down the hall, straight to the nurses' station. Richard followed quickly behind him.

Kendra Camp came out from the nurses' station and met Hank. "Mrs. Redman's in surgery. They rushed her in there about ten minutes ago."

"Tell me what you know. Please." Hank balled his hands into fists. His jaw tightened. A fine mist glazed his eyes.

"Come on down to the waiting room." Kendra laced her arm through Hank's, then glanced over her shoulder and nodded at Richard. "I'll tell you what I know."

They reached the waiting room in a matter of minutes. A small room with pale green walls and vinyl furniture.

"Why don't we sit down," Kendra suggested.

"I can't sit," Hank said. "Tell me. How bad is it? And what are her chances?"

Kendra glanced nervously at Richard. "There's a lot of internal bleeding and her pregnancy complicates matters. Dr. Hall and Dr. Farr are both in the operating room." Kendra took Hank's hands in hers. "There's a good chance that they'll have to perform an emergency C-section."

"A C-section? But she's not even seven months pregnant," Hank said. "It's too soon for the baby to be born."

Kendra squeezed Hank's hands. "Premature infants have a much better chance of survival now than they once did. If—and I'm saying if—they have to take the baby, then we'll rush him straight to the neonatal unit. We have a fine one here at County General. And if necessary, we can med-flight him straight to Nashville."

"She can't lose her baby," Hank said. "You don't know what that child means to her."

"I understand." Kendra's eyes filled with tears. "I know it's all she has left of her husband. Believe me, the doctors will do everything they can to save both her and the baby."

Hank wanted to shout from the rooftops—*Not Lowell's*

baby! My baby! My son! "Are you saying it might come down to saving either her or the child?"

"Try not to think about—"

Hank flung off Kendra's hands and glared at her. "Dammit, tell me!"

"Yes. If they decide to do the C-section, it might endanger the child, but it could save Susan's life."

"Then tell them to do the Caesarean." Hank grabbed Kendra's shoulders. "Do you hear me? Go in there and tell them that Susan comes first. They have to save her."

"Oh, Hank." Tears trickled down Kendra's face.

"Hank, she can't go into the operating room and tell the doctors what to do," Richard said as he placed his hand on Hank's shoulder. "Besides, even if she could, they can't take orders from you. You aren't Susan's husband and you're not her baby's father."

"I'm not Susan's husband, yet." Hank jerked away from his deputy, turned and looked first at Richard and then at Kendra. "But she's going to marry me. Just as soon as possible. She's my fiancée. Doesn't that count for something?"

"Oh, Hank, I realize how much you care about her, but—" Kendra said.

"I love her." The depth of his feelings for Susan came into clear focus for him. He did love her—more than anything on earth. "And if anyone has a right to make decisions about Susan's child, I do. I gave Lowell and her that baby. But Lowell's gone now. And by God, I am not going to let Susan die, too. Do you hear me?"

"Hank, you're upset and confused." Richard glanced nervously at Kendra, and Hank knew what the two of them were thinking—that he'd lost his mind.

"I'm the father of Susan's baby," Hank said.

Kendra gasped. Total silence filled the waiting area. The

dead silence ended a few seconds later, when Caleb and Sheila Bishop entered the room.

"We got here as quick as we could." Sheila wrapped her arms around Hank and hugged him.

"Thank goodness, y'all are here," Kendra said. "I'm afraid Hank's pretty upset and he—"

"Kendra and Richard think I've gone nuts," Hank said.

"He's not crazy," Caleb assured them. "He is the father of Susan's baby." Caleb glanced at his big brother, his gaze questioning him, asking permission to explain the situation.

"Lowell was sterile," Hank said. "I donated my sperm so Susan could be artificially inseminated. That baby she's carrying is mine."

"I'll get word to Dr. Farr," Kendra said, then hurried off down the hall.

Richard Holman slumped down in a nearby chair. "I knew Lowell and Susan had been trying to have a baby for nearly a year and that they'd gone to all kinds of specialists, but I had no idea that they'd…that the baby was… Damn!"

"How is Susan?" Sheila asked as she led Hank over to the green vinyl sofa. "Let's sit down."

Hank followed her suggestion and they both sat. "Internal bleeding. That's about all I know. They're operating now. And…there's a chance they might have to do an emergency C-section. It may come down to deciding whether to save Susan or save the baby."

"Oh, dear God," Sheila said, her voice a gasping sob.

"I'd better call Tallie," Caleb said.

"Yes," Sheila agreed. "And we need to let Donna know before she finds out from someone else."

Hank couldn't sit still. He twisted and turned on the sofa for several minutes and then he got up and paced around the room. He felt as if he were locked in a cage. He wanted to run—hard and fast—and escape from the possibility that he might lose Susan. And the baby.

Don't do this! He prayed silently. *Not when Susan and I finally have a chance at real happiness. Don't take her away from me. Please, let her live. And let our son live. I promise that I'll be the best husband and the best father I know how to be. I'll never let them down. I swear!*

Tears gathered heavily in Hank's eyes. Drops trailed down his face, over his jaw and onto his neck. He hadn't cried since he'd been a kid. Six. Maybe seven. He hadn't cried when his grandfather died. He hadn't even cried when Lowell died, and he'd loved Lowell like a brother. But this was Susan. His Susan. The woman who loved him.

Minutes ticked by. As he paced the floor, Hank occasionally glanced at the wall clock. The telephone in the waiting area rang continuously—people calling to check on Susan's condition. Sheila took all the calls, whispering her replies. Hank realized she didn't want him to hear her repeating the same answers over and over again. With every step, every breath, Hank prayed.

Thirty minutes later, Donna Fields, round from head to toe and with swollen hands and feet, waddled into the waiting room. She hugged Hank, but didn't say anything. Her eyes were red and swollen and clouded with fresh tears. She turned to Sheila. The two embraced and then sat together on the vinyl sofa.

Three hours later the waiting room was filled to capacity. Tallie and Peyton. Mrs. Dobson and Mrs. Brown. Sheila's brother Mike and his wife. Scooter Bellamy and his mother. Crooked Oak's mayor and a dozen assorted friends, including Peyton's brother Spence and his wife Pattie.

"The whole county is praying for Susan, my boy," Reverend Swan said. "It's all in God's hands now."

Time became meaningless. People spoke to him, hugged him, patted him on the back and shook his hand. He tried to respond, but the best he could manage was a blank stare. It took every ounce of his willpower to keep his emotions under control. He wanted to shout out his anger and vent his frustration by ripping apart half the world. But all he could do was wait. Wait to find out if after today he'd have a reason to go on living.

The crowd inside the waiting room stilled suddenly, their voices becoming silent. Hank sensed the change in the atmosphere. He looked around and there stood Dr. Farr just outside the doorway. The crowd parted as Hank rushed toward Susan's obstetrician.

"We performed the Caesarean and took the baby," Dr. Farr said. "He's small—just barely three pounds." Dr. Farr placed his hand on Hank's shoulder. "He's upstairs on third in the neonatal unit."

"How is he?" Hank asked. "What...are his chances?"

"All things considered, we're lucky," Dr. Farr said. "There's a good chance your son will live, but it's too soon to make any predictions. If you'd like, you can go up and see him."

Hank grabbed the doctor's arm. "What about Susan?"

"Dr. Hall will come out and talk to you soon."

Caleb walked up beside Hank. "Susan's going to be all right. You've got to keep telling yourself that and believe it."

"She was so upset with me this morning," Hank said. "I asked her to marry me, but I went about it all wrong. I didn't even tell her that I loved her. Hell—" Hank raked his fingers through his hair "—this morning, I didn't realize I loved her so damn much!"

"Don't do this to yourself. Susan's going to live and you'll get a chance to tell her how you feel."

"I've been such a stubborn jackass. I've put her through a lot of misery because I was too frigging scared of marriage and fatherhood and lifetime commitments."

"Susan understood," Caleb said. "And she'll forgive you. Look what I put Sheila through and she forgave me."

"God, I just hope I get the chance to ask her to forgive me." *And to tell her that I love her. That she is my life.*

A few minutes later Dr. Hall found Hank and Caleb walking the halls of the second floor. Hank froze on the spot. For one terrifying moment he thought Susan was dead.

"Susan's in SICU," Dr. Hall said. "I'm sure Dr. Farr has told you that she came through the C-section just fine. We've done all we can for her. We've stopped the internal bleeding and—"

"Is she going to live?" Hank asked.

"I don't know," Dr. Hall replied. "The next twenty-four to forty-eight hours are critical. If she makes it through the night, I'd say she has a good chance of surviving."

"May I see her?"

Dr. Hall nodded. "I'll tell the SICU nurses to let you go in and stay with her for a few minutes."

"Thanks." Hank shook the doctor's hand, then turned to his brother, "Would you explain the situation to Sheila and Donna...and everybody?"

"Sure thing," Caleb replied. "You go on and see Susan. I'll take care of things here."

Hank hesitated at the SICU entrance. *Susan is going to be fine. Susan is going to be fine.* He repeated the sentence as if it were a litany, a holy chant that would protect her from death. He opened the door, walked in and looked around at the numerous enclosed cubicles.

A heavy-set, middle-aged nurse came up to him. "Sheriff Bishop, Mrs. Redman is in Number Four. Follow me."

Hank's stomach knotted painfully as he entered the room. Susan lay quiet and still, her face bruised, cut and swollen, her body attached to an assortment of wires and tubes. She looked very small and completely helpless.

"Dr. Hall said you could stay ten minutes," the nurse

said. "Then you can come back at the regular visiting times."

Hank nodded, then moved closer to the bed. He hovered over Susan, willing her to live. He lifted her lifeless little hand and brought it to his lips. After kissing her hand tenderly, he pressed it against his cheek.

"There's something I want you to know," he said. "I love you, Susan. Do you hear me? I love you."

She didn't stir. No movement except the undulation of her chest as she breathed.

"You've got to get well, honey. Our son needs his mother. He's upstairs right now, getting the best care in the world. Dr. Farr said he's just fine. He's small, but he's going to make it." Just a little white lie, Hank told himself. Just a half-truth.

Hank stayed at her side, talking to her, encouraging her, repeatedly telling her how much he loved her.

The nurse standing in the doorway cleared her throat. "You'll have to leave now, Sheriff. But you can come back in a couple of hours at the next regular visiting time."

Hank leaned over, kissed Susan's forehead and then left the room. His family waited for him just outside the SICU entrance, in the tiny visitors' area.

"How was she?" Sheila asked.

"Asleep," Hank replied. "I can go back in and see her in two hours."

"How about some lunch?" Caleb suggested. "We can all go grab a bite in the cafeteria."

"I want to see my son," Hank said.

Tears misted Sheila's and Tallie's eyes. The two women slipped their arms through Hank's, flanking him.

"Let's all go up and see my nephew," Tallie said. "They might not let us all in, but we can peep through the door."

The staff suited Hank in green hospital garb that included

a face mask, then allowed him into the neonatal unit. His son lay in an incubator, his tiny body connected to countless tubes and wires, just as his mother's body was similarly connected to life-saving equipment on the floor below.

His son had perfect little arms and legs. Ten fingers and ten toes. A round head covered with dark fuzz.

A feeling like none he'd ever known overwhelmed Hank. That tiny little thing lying there, fighting for life, was his son. His and Susan's child. Conceived as the ultimate repayment to a friend. A child he had never planned to be a father to in any way.

"You keep on fighting, son. Do you hear me? I'm your father. And don't think for one minute that I don't want you or love you, because I do. God, I do. I do." Tears streamed down Hank's face. His shoulders shook with his attempt at controlling the sobs.

"You've got to live for your mother and me. She's downstairs right now, fighting just as hard as you are. And when she wakes up, the first thing she's going to ask me is how you're doing. I want to be able to tell her that you're all right."

With these words, Hank left the neonatal unit, ran past his family and into the nearest men's room. He leaned his head against the wall in the empty room for a couple of minutes, struggling to bring his emotions under control.

When Caleb and Peyton entered the rest room, Hank was washing his face with a wet paper towel. He blew his nose, tossed the towel into the trash and took a deep breath.

"Anything we can do?" Peyton asked.

"I'm okay," Hank said. "I just needed a few minutes to, er, to—"

"How about some lunch now?" Caleb said. "You still have about an hour before you can go back in to see Susan again."

"Yeah, sure," Hank said. "I could use some coffee."

* * *

When Hank returned to the SICU, he found Susan still asleep. He asked the nurses why she hadn't awakened and they told him, reluctantly, that Susan was in a coma.

He stayed at the hospital all day and all night. Waiting, praying, and hoping beyond hope that Susan would awaken. He made several trips upstairs to check on his son. The boy was a fighter, they told him. His son was hanging on.

People came and went. Everyone was concerned. All their friends were supportive and caring. He spoke to the doctors numerous times. Each time he was told all that could be done was being done—for Susan and their child. Dr. Hall was cautiously optimistic about Susan's recovery, but he was concerned that she still remained in a coma. And only time could save their son. Each day he survived, he would—hopefully—grow stronger.

Caleb brought Hank a change of clothes the second day. Three day's beard stubble covered Hank's face. And after sleeping on the sofa in the waiting room every night, Hank's body felt as if it had been beaten.

Seventy hours after Susan had been placed in SICU, the nurse came out into the waiting area and woke Hank from a nap. She shook his shoulder. "Sheriff Bishop?"

His eyelids flew open. He stared up at the nurse. "What is it? What's wrong?"

"Nothing's wrong," she assured him. "Dr. Hall is with Mrs. Redman. She's regained consciousness."

Hank raced into the SICU, straight to Number Four.

"There he is," Dr. Hall said to Susan, then turned to Hank. "She's been asking for you."

Hank went to her, the happiness inside him near the bursting point. She lifted her hand. He grabbed it, kissed it and held it tenderly.

"Our baby?" she asked.

Hank glanced back at Dr. Hall, who nodded affirmatively. "He's upstairs in the neonatal unit. He's little. Just barely three pounds. But he's fully developed—his lungs and all. He's on a respirator, but they think they'll be able to take him off of it in another day or two. He's got ten toes and fingers, with toenails and fingernails. And a lot of dark fuzz on his head."

"I want to see him," Susan said.

"Susan, you're not quite ready to get out of bed yet, let alone make a trip upstairs," Dr. Hall told her. "You'll have to let Hank keep you updated for a few more days."

"But I'm all right, aren't I? I want to see my baby." Tears clouded Susan's eyes.

Hank brought her hand to his lips and kissed her knuckles repeatedly. "Just as soon as you're able to, I'll take you upstairs to see him. I promise."

"The best thing you can do for your son is to get well yourself," Dr. Hall said. "Hank can stay with you for as long as you'd like. And we just might move you out into a private room in the morning."

Hank pulled up a chair and sat beside Susan's bed. She turned and took a good look at him.

"You look terrible," she said. "How long has it been since you got some sleep?"

"I've taken a few naps over the past three days."

"Have I been here three days?"

"Three and a half."

"Oh, Hank, you should have gone home and gotten some sleep." She ran her fingertips over his beard stubble. "And you should have shaved."

"What's the matter, don't you like my beard?"

"Why didn't you go home?"

"How can you ask me that?" He leaned over and kissed her. "I couldn't leave you and our son here at the hospital.

If I'd been the one lying here unconscious, would you have left me?''

"No, but I love—"

"And I love you, Susan." He cupped her face gently with his hands. "I love you."

"You love me?"

"Yes, I do. And I want you to marry me. You know what I was fixing to do when I got word that you'd been in an accident?''

"No, what were you fixing to do?"

"Make reservations for dinner, order you some flowers, and buy you an engagement ring."

"Oh, Hank. I thought when you said…all you talked about was duty and responsibility and doing the right thing. You never mentioned that you loved me."

"Yeah, well, I'm an idiot. I didn't handle things the right way and I realize that I went about proposing to you all wrong. I'm not much of a bargain, honey. I'm not as good a man as Lowell. He was kind and gentle and easygoing and would have been—"

Susan covered his lips with her fingers. "Shh-hh. I loved Lowell. I know what a wonderful man he was. And I think we should name our son after him. But you're the man I've been in love with since I was a teenager. You're the man I've always wanted."

"I think naming our son after Lowell is a good idea. Lowell would have liked that, wouldn't he?"

"He would have understood our being in love, too," Susan said. "He would have wanted us to be together. You and me and little Lowell Redman Bishop."

"He's going to make it," Hank said. "We're not going to lose our son."

The next day Susan was moved into a private room, and two days later Hank pushed her wheelchair into the neonatal unit to see her son for the first time.

"Come take a look at him," the nurse said. "We took him off the ventilator four hours ago and he's breathing just fine on his own. He's gaining weight already and we're betting you'll get to take little Lowell home in a few weeks."

Indescribable joy welled up inside Susan. Joy beyond any she'd ever experienced before in her life. She looked at her son, Hank's son, and her heart filled with gratitude.

"Hello, Lowell, I'm your mother. You and I have a little catching up to do."

They stayed with their son for over an hour, until Susan began to tire. Hank promised they'd return again, later that afternoon.

"I love you, darling," Susan told her son. "Mommy's here for you. For the rest of your life."

"I love you, son," Hank said. "And I'm going to be around for you, too. We're going to go hunting and fishing and play baseball together. And you're going to help me take care of your mother and make sure she's happy."

Hank leaned over, kissed Susan and then wheeled her out into the hallway. When they returned to her room, they found it filled with people—friends and relatives packed the room and lined the hallway.

"Since you missed your baby shower, we decided to bring it to you," Sheila said. "I checked with Dr. Hall and he said he thought you might be up to a little party, as long as we didn't stay too long."

One by one, Susan's friends brought their gifts to her and she opened each with love. After the last present had been stacked in a large box Sheila had provided, Susan reached out for Hank's hand.

"We have an announcement to make," she said as Hank took her hand in his.

"Hank and I are going to get married as soon as little Lowell is able to leave the hospital."

Congratulations began, but before the well-wishers went any further, Susan cleared her throat. Everyone stopped talking all at once.

"I think there's something y'all should know. Hank's family already knows, but...well, I want all our friends to know the truth." Susan took a deep breath. *Oh, Lowell, this is the right thing to do. I know you understand.* "Lowell was sterile, but he wanted to give me a child. So he asked his best friend to donate sperm so that I could be artificially inseminated. If Lowell had lived, the baby would have been ours—always. But the truth is that Hank is my son's biological father."

Hank knew how much courage it had taken her to face her friends and tell them the truth. He didn't think he could ever love her more than he did at that very minute. He knew he probably didn't deserve Susan, but that fact sure wasn't going to keep him from marrying her and spending the rest of his life trying to be worthy of her.

Epilogue

Lowell Redman Bishop's parents brought him home from the hospital when he was five weeks and four days old. He weighed a whopping five pounds, one ounce—the combined result, the doctors said, of his huge appetite and the constant love and care of his mother and father. Everyone agreed that little Lowell was Hank's spitting image—black hair and brown eyes and a very stubborn chin.

Today Susan had dressed him in a white one-piece outfit and a matching bonnet, which was almost too large for his tiny head. She wrapped him in a white blanket that Mrs. Dobson had hand crocheted and handed over her pride and joy to his "Aunt" Donna for the duration of the wedding ceremony.

Hank and Susan had agreed that they wanted their union to be shared by only their family and closest friends. Donna had helped Susan plan the event and she had organized everything, despite the fact that her baby was due at any time. Sheila and Tallie had done most of the physical work required to turn the front parlor of Susan's home into the setting for her wedding. Cream roses, baby's breath and white lilies filled the house. Satin bows decorated chairs, tables and mantel. Crystal candleholders filled with white and cream candles of every size created a warm glow.

Susan took a deep breath when she heard the music begin. This was the moment she had been waiting for all her life. The day she would marry the man she loved—Hank Bishop.

Her whole life had changed in recent months and would change even more when she and little Lowell moved to Virginia with Hank, after his term as sheriff ended. She wasn't sure how she'd like living so far away from her home and her friends, but she knew she'd make any sacrifice for Hank. He had a career with the FBI and she would never ask him to permanently give up a job he loved. After all, what really mattered was that they would be together— she and her husband and son. And of course, they were taking Lucy, Ethel, Fred and Ricky with them when they moved. Hank complained about the *mutts* and *felines,* but she knew they were beginning to win him over.

Susan took one last look at the mirror in the upstairs hallway. The bruises were gone and the makeup covered the faint lines left from the healing scars on the side of her face. Donna had swept her hair up into a French twist, making her look far more sophisticated than she was. She had decided against a typical wedding dress. After all, this was her second marriage. Instead, she had chosen a cream silk dress. Draped across the shoulders. Fitted at the waist. Flowing from her hips to mid-calf. Simple and elegant. Her only ornamentation, besides the emerald-cut diamond engagement ring Hank had given her, was her aunt Alice's pearl necklace.

Governor Peyton Rand offered her his arm. She smiled

at Tallie's husband and laced her arm through his. Tallie and Sheila, costumed in springtime dresses of pale yellow chiffon, preceded her down the stairs and into the front parlor. Peyton led her to where Hank waited with Reverend Swan. Hank stood in front of the fireplace, which was decorated with garlands of roses and lilies. He wore a new black suit and a gray and maroon striped tie. Without a doubt, he was the handsomest man alive.

With his brother Caleb at his side, Hank turned to her, the smile on his face telling her how happy he was. As Sheila and Tallie took their places at her side, Donna came and joined them, holding baby Lowell in her arms.

"Dearly Beloved," Reverend Swan began the ceremony.

The day was perfect, Susan thought as she and Hank exchanged their vows. A dream come true because two people had overcome their fears and self-doubts and taken a chance on love.

"I now pronounce you man and wife," the minister proclaimed. "Hank, you may kiss your bride."

The kiss was deeply intimate and sealed their passionate love. Caleb cleared his throat. Tallie laughed. When Hank finally released her, they turned to face their friends.

Donna had arranged for a caterer to prepare the reception and everything was set up to perfection in the dining room. Standing side by side, Susan and Hank cut their wedding cake, while a local photographer took their picture.

Suddenly, Tallie cried from the hallway, then burst into laughter. "My God, Jake! I can't believe you actually came. You're too late for the wedding, but the reception's just starting."

"You don't mean our big brother actually came home for your wedding," Caleb said to Hank. "Will wonders never cease. He didn't bother making the trip for Tallie's wedding or mine."

"I'll be damned," Hank said. "It is Jake!"

"Well, this does make the day perfect, doesn't it?" Susan said. "All three Bishop brothers together for the first time in…how long?"

"Seventeen years," Hank said, slipping his arm around Susan's waist and leading her over to meet the new arrival.

"You old son of a gun," Jake Bishop said, slapping Hank on the back. "You said you'd never get married or have any kids, but from what Caleb tells me, you've done both. This gal must be something special to trap my little brother."

"Honey, I'd like for you to meet the black sheep of the family, my big brother, Jake."

Susan reached out and hugged Jake. He grinned from ear to ear, then kissed the bride on the cheek. "You're a lucky man," Jake said. "How about introducing me to my nephews? I've got another one now, don't I? At least that's what Caleb told me when I called him yesterday."

Susan turned to ask Donna to bring Lowell over to meet his uncle, but Donna had disappeared into another room. Danny, Caleb's son, held his little cousin. Susan motioned to him.

Jake lifted the child out of Danny's arms and held him up for inspection. "Well, he's a Bishop, all right." He ruffled Danny's hair. "And so are you, son." Jake laughed heartily. "A second generation of Bishops. Lord help us all."

"Amen to that. Now, give me that baby before you drop him!" Tallie scooped up little Lowell. "Come on everybody, we've got a reception going on here. Music. Food. Champagne."

Hank pulled Susan off into the hallway, into a quiet, private corner, then backed her up against the wall. "I love you, Mrs. Bishop."

"And I love you, Mr. Bishop." She caressed his cheek.

"I'm sorry we have to postpone our honeymoon, but until Lowell's a little bigger and I've completely recovered—"

Hank covered her mouth with his, robbing her of her breath and of all coherent thought. Every time he touched her, rockets went off inside her. Hank always made her feel this way. Only Hank.

"Dr. Hall and Dr. Farr did say that we could have a wedding night, didn't they?" Hank cupped her hips and pulled her up against him.

She draped her arms around his neck. "Oh, yes, they most certainly did."

"Then come on, honey, let's get this reception over with so we can get started on the fun part of being married."

"Let's go," she agreed.

And then Mr. and Mrs. Hank Bishop joined their family and friends, and began their life as a happily married couple.

* * * * *

Don't miss
HAVING HIS BABY,
book 3 of Beverly Barton's emotional series,
3 BABIES FOR 3 BROTHERS,
coming next month,
only from Silhouette Desire!

SILHOUETTE
DESIRE ®

AVAILABLE FROM 21ST APRIL 2000

RIO: MAN OF DESTINY Cait London

Man of the Month & The Blaylocks

Rio Blaylock craved babies and a loving wife. But the one woman he wanted had just inherited half his business, and marriage was the last thing on independent Paloma Forbes's mind. So how could Rio show Paloma that he was the one for her?

HAVING HIS BABY Beverly Barton

3 Babies for 3 Brothers

Jake Bishop was a daddy! One look at his tiny daughter and he wanted to be a full-time parent. But beautiful Donna Fields had different ideas. Could Jake convince the mother of his child he was just the man she needed?

BLACKHAWK'S SWEET REVENGE
Barbara McCauley

Secrets

Lucas Blackhawk was back in town, and seeking revenge. Julianna Hadley boldly agreed to his shocking proposal. She would marry him! And this virgin bride resolved to win all of Blackhawk's heart!

MUM IN WAITING Maureen Child

Bachelor Battalion

To be the belle of her school reunion Tracy Hall needed a glamorous makeover *and* a fiancé! Who better than Marine captain Rick Bennet? But after their unexpected night of passion, Tracy *was* expecting…

THE WILFUL WIFE Suzanne Simms

Detective Mathis Hazard took one look at lovely hotel owner Desiree Stratford and suddenly became enthusiastic about his new case! Especially when he decided to pretend to be Desiree's husband…

THE BRIDAL PROMISE Virginia Dove

Twelve years ago, lies drove lovers Matt Ransom and Perri Stone apart. Now forced into marriage and with a child on the way, can the truth heal these two wounded hearts?

0004/22a

Welcome back to the drama and mystery that is the Fortune Dynasty.

A Fortune's Children Wedding is coming to you at a special price of only £3.99 and contains a money off coupon for issue one of *Fortune's Children Brides*.

With issue one priced at a special introductory offer of 99p you can get it **FREE** with your money off coupon.

Published 24 March 2000

Published 21 April 2000

Published 19 May 2000

Available at most branches of WH Smith, Tesco, Tesco Ireland, Martins, RS McCall, Forbuoys, Borders, Easons, and other leading bookshops

AVAILABLE FROM 21ST APRIL 2000

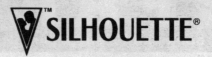

2 FREE

books and a surprise gift!

We would like to take this opportunity to thank you for reading this Silhouette® book by offering you the chance to take TWO more specially selected titles from the Desire™ series absolutely FREE! We're also making this offer to introduce you to the benefits of the Reader Service™—

★ FREE home delivery
★ FREE gifts and competitions
★ FREE monthly Newsletter
★ Exclusive Reader Service discounts
★ Books available before they're in the shops

Accepting these FREE books and gift places you under no obligation to buy, you may cancel at any time, even after receiving your free shipment. Simply complete your details below and return the entire page to the address below. *You don't even need a stamp!*

YES! Please send me 2 free Desire books and a surprise gift. I understand that unless you hear from me, I will receive 4 superb new titles every month for just £2.70 each, postage and packing free. I am under no obligation to purchase any books and may cancel my subscription at any time. The free books and gift will be mine to keep in any case.

D0EA

Ms/Mrs/Miss/Mr ....Initials................................
BLOCK CAPITALS PLEASE

Surname ....

Address ....

....

....Postcode................................

Send this whole page to:
UK: FREEPOST CN81, Croydon, CR9 3WZ
EIRE: PO Box 4546, Kilcock, County Kildare (stamp required)

Men who can't be tamed by just *any* woman!

We know you'll love our selection of the most passionate and adventurous Sensation™ hero every month as the Heartbreaker.

HEARTBREAKERS